Also by Paige Dixon

May I Cross Your Golden River?
Lion on the Mountain
Silver Wolf
The Young Grizzly
Promises to Keep

The Search
for Charlie

PAIGE DIXON

The Search for Charlie

Atheneum NEW YORK 1976

To Ben Irwin

LIBRARY OF CONGRESS
CATALOGING IN PUBLICATION DATA

Dixon, Paige.   The search for Charlie.

SUMMARY: Accompanied by an Indian friend,
a girl pursues her young brother's
kidnapper through the forest of Montana.
[1. Montana—Fiction]   I. Title.
PZ7.D6457Se   [Fic]   75-23187
ISBN 0-689-30500-1

The Search
for Charlie

Jane lay on her stomach on the big sheepskin rug, a geology book propped up in front of her, books and notes scattered around her. Somebody knocked on the door and said, "Janey? Coffee?"

"No, thanks," Jane said abstractedly. "Got an exam tomorrow."

"Okay." The footsteps moved down the hall.

Jane shoved her glasses up on her nose and reread the paragraph she had just finished. She liked geology, but it was tough, and she had to work to get her *B*. Identification really bugged her. Aloud, she said, "Ecologite: a rock consisting of granular aggregate of green pyroxene and red garnet, often having also cyanite, silvery mica, quartz, and pyrite." She flipped the pages of her notes to a list and read, "Cyanite: a mineral aluminum silicate, Al_2SiO_5, occurring in blue or greenish bladed crystals, used as a refractory."

She got up and went to the window, repeating to herself what she had just read. All right, let that go for now. How about the Jurassic period—did it follow the Triassic and precede the Cretaceous, or vice versa? Followed the Triassic. All right, memorize the initials—T J C—*T* for the Tetons, *J* for Jane, *C* for Charlie.

She smiled. It was a cinch; she only had to remember the trip her parents and her little brother Charlie and she had taken to the Tetons during the summer. If she got a good grade on the exam, she'd tell Charlie how she used him to remember the right answer. He'd laugh.

She pushed open the casement window and looked out at Lake Waban. Some girls in a canoe paddled slowly across the gray water. The sky was cloudy, but the early October foliage was reflected in the lake in fainter colors. It was pretty in an altogether different way from her own western Montana. She liked Massachusetts, but there were many moments when she ached with homesickness for the ranch and the mountains and her family, especially Charlie. There were enough years between them so they had never had to be competitive, and yet their temperaments were similar enough to make them good friends.

Well, back to work. She bit into an apple and stretched out on the floor again. But in a few minutes there was a quick knock and the door opened.

"Janey, knock it off. Walk to the Vil with me. I need nourishment."

"Can't do it, Sadie. I've got to study."

Sadie made a face. "You're too single-minded. Where's it going to get you?"

Jane smiled at her friend. "Ahead."

"That dinner was one of the worst, I mean *thee-ee* worst. I'm starving."

"Have an apple."

"Apple. What I need is a steak. I'll settle for a hamburger. Want me to bring you one?"

"Yeah, will you? There's some change on the desk.

Thanks, kid."

"It's nothing. I live but to serve you. Coffee, too?"

"With cream and one sugar."

"I know, don't rub it in. I hate girls with figures like yours. Hate them, hate them." Sadie patted her plump stomach. "I think thin, but I come out fat." She took some money from the desk. "See you."

"Tally-ho."

When the door was closed, Jane put her fists against her temples and tried to concentrate over the noise of voices in the corridor, telephone ringing, somebody's stereo. Triassic: earliest period of the Mesozoic; characterized by widespread land deposits; follows Permian, precedes . . . precedes Jane. Jane for Jurassic. What's *P*? Pop? Pop, Tetons, Jane, Charlie. Where's Mother? Oh, of course, Mesozoic. Oh, God, I'm getting myself all messed up. Permian, latest Paleozoic, follows Pennsylvania—what a lovely collection of *P*'s—characterized by salt deposits, and glacial activity in the southern hemisphere. I never learned to study, that's my problem, even after a year of college I still don't study right. Ought to be able to cram those facts into my stupid skull. Daddy has total recall, why couldn't I have inherited it? No organization. For instance, why am I learning the geological periods backwards? No sense of order.

She worked for about an hour, shutting everything else out of her mind. Then she got up and stretched and put her head out the window for some fresh air. It was getting dark. Days were getting shorter. Winter coming on. She had the rancher's habit of thinking in terms of weather. Sadie said she was a spoilsport, talking

5

about winter when it was only early October and the whole countryside shining with color.

"Open up, open up. I come bearing nourishment." Sadie kicked open the door, her hands full of paper bags. "Oliver sends you his love, and he put in an extra pickle for you." She put the bags on the desk.

"I'm famished." Jane took out the hamburger and bit into it. "Mmmm. Oliver's got the gourmet touch."

The phone at the end of the hall rang.

"I'd better get that," Sadie said. "Steve said he'd call." As she opened the door, the phone stopped ringing. She stood listening while someone else answered. "Who's it for, Pat?"

"Janey."

"It's for you, Jane. Maybe it's that cute guy you met in Cambridge."

Jane ran down the hall to the phone booth and picked up the phone.

"It's long distance," Pat said to her. "Person-to-person."

"Hello? . . . Yes, I'm Jane Worden. . . . Daddy? Hi! How are you? What's up?" She stopped smiling. "What? Say it again, Daddy, slowly. . . . Well, what does the sheriff say? Don't they say *anything*? . . . I'll be there as fast as I can get there. Hold on tight, Daddy. Tell Mom . . ." Her voice broke, and she hung up.

When she came into her room, Sadie said, "Was it the guy from . . ." She broke off. "Janey, what's the matter?"

"Something's happened to my brother." Jane sat down abruptly on her bed.

"To Charlie? What's happened?"

"He's gone."

"My God! Do you mean he's dead?"

"No, no. He's gone. Disappeared. The police think he was kidnapped."

"Oh, no!" She moved toward Jane, but Jane got up suddenly and ran to her closet. "I've got to pack and get to the airport. Will you call me a cab?"

"I'll take you myself. Listen, while you pack, I'll go clear it with the housemother." As Sadie left the room, she called, "Pat, call the airport and see what Jane can get right away for Montana." She put her head back in the door. "What airport do you want to go to, Jane?"

Jane was throwing clothes into a suitcase. "Kalispell. Or Missoula. Whichever they can get." Sadie disappeared, and Jane paused, staring unseeingly into her suitcase. No, no, no, nothing could happen to Charlie. She wouldn't allow it. She would not stand for it. As soon as she got there, she'd find him, and he'd be all right. Nothing else was thinkable.

Sadie drove fast and skillfully, not talking. When she parked in the limited zone at Logan airport, and a porter told her she couldn't leave the car there unattended, she spoke to him quietly and quickly. Then, following Jane to the ticket window, she took Jane's purse and said, "Sit down. I'll get the ticket." In a few minutes she arrived where Jane was sitting, with the ticket.

"Gate 6. It'll board in twenty minutes. You change at Chicago."

"Good," Jane said. "Thanks, Sadie." She looked at her friend. "I think he's just wandered off and gotten interested in something, the way he does. By the time I get there, he'll probably be home."

"Sure. Well, it'll give you a break from classes."

"They don't know much of anything at all. It's probably just the sheriff wanting a little excitement in his life so he decides it's a kidnapping." She tried to laugh. "You eastern dudes think you're the only ones with interesting crimes."

Sadie laughed a little too heartily. "Right. You guys are trying to compete, that's all."

Jane looked in the mirror of her purse and combed

her hair. "I look wild."

"You look fine."

"They found a note, but they can't read it."

"Why not? Can't your cops read?"

"It sounds like a bad movie. The note was stuck to the front door with Scotch tape but it had rained and the words were blurred."

Sadie looked scared. "There was really a note?"

"But they can't read it. I'll bet one of Charlie's crazy friends thought it was a good joke."

"Maybe Charlie himself . . ."

"No, he's got better sense than that. He would know we'd be scared. It might be that Ellis kid—he's kind of a nut. Or . . ." She tried to think of someone.

"Maybe that Indian kid you've told me about?"

"Vic? No, he'd never do a thing like that. Vic is very serious and responsible. He loves Charlie."

The sepulchral voice on the loudspeaker announced that the flight Jane was taking would be boarding in ten minutes. Sadie walked with her as far as the electronic inspection point.

"Listen, Janey," she said, speaking quickly, "if you need me, whistle. For anything at all. I think things'll be all right. Don't worry about things till you know if there's anything to worry about. Just hang tough."

Jane shook hands with her almost formally. "Thanks an awful lot." She went through the checkpoint and hurried on down the corridor, not looking back.

She got a window seat, and was relieved when no one took the aisle seat. She didn't want to talk to anyone. She wanted to think about something absolutely impersonal and think about it very hard. She decided to review the geologic periods. Slowly and methodically, as the plane took off and flew low over the water of the harbor, she ticked off in her mind the successive periods and their characteristics. Then she started doing types of rock formation, trying to see the lab samples in her mind as she named them. She'd have to make up the exam when she got back, so she might as well be ready.

At Chicago she had to change to another airline. She bought a newspaper and on the plane, read it impatiently, as if she were looking for something. But of course, there was nothing in it about Charlie. What did they know or care about Charlie in Chicago. If it had turned out to be a real kidnapping, though, it would make the national press, wouldn't it, she asked herself. Maybe it was a good sign that there wasn't anything in the paper. She began to go over Italian verbs. She was majoring in modern languages, and Signorina got annoyed with her because sometimes she mixed up Spanish and Italian.

It was very black outside the plane, with clouds below. The stewardess came around with sandwiches and coffee. The plane was half empty and the people sitting near Jane were nearly all asleep. When she had finished her sandwich, she tried to sleep too, but it didn't work. She gave up finally and sat up, staring out into the blackness. Don't let anything happen to Charlie. *Don't let anything happen to Charlie.*

When the plane angled northwest from Denver, Jane kept her face against the cold window, trying to make out the form of the Rockies; but an occasional glimpse of vague, almost menacing shapes rising above the clouds here and there was all she could get.

Coming across the Divide in Montana, the plane flew lower and the moon lit a few mountain peaks, usually reassuring to her; but now they merely loomed black and forbidding below the plane. She remembered laughing at Sadie's fear of them, when Sadie had flown home with her last year for spring vacation. "Good grief!" Sadie had said. "What if we crash? It'd be like crashing on the moon." For the first time in her life the mountains now seemed frightening to her, too. Perhaps it was because she had never flown over them at night before.

The airport was deserted except for a sleepy-looking clerk, and a taxi driver who looked as if he hoped no one would come. She was the only passenger getting off, but still she felt nervous lest someone get the taxi away from her.

She hurried up to the driver and told him where she wanted to go.

"Young lady," he said, "that's twenty-five miles away."

"I know. But I have to get home."

"If you wait till morning, you can catch the Intermountain bus."

"I can't wait till morning." She began to feel panicky. "Look, I'll pay you extra."

Still he hesitated. He was a frail-looking, elderly man, with most of his teeth gone. He looked sick. "I don't hardly see my way clear to going way out there, this time of night."

"Please. I've got to get there. My little brother is lost."

"Lost?"

"I've just flown in from Massachusetts. My brother is missing. He might be kidnapped." She hated saying it, because it made it seem more possible.

But it had its effect. The man looked interested. "Do you mean that rancher's boy? The Worden boy?"

"Yes. I'm Jane Worden."

"You go get in the cab," he said. "I'll bring your luggage."

It frightened her that he knew about it. That meant it had been in the news. It meant Charlie hadn't been found. She got into the taxi, trying to control the sudden wave of nausea that hit her.

The man came out in a few minutes with her bag, put it in the trunk, and slammed the lid down. The taxi was old. Jane hoped it wouldn't break down.

He drove out of the airport and onto the highway with more speed and skill than she had expected. Toothless or not, he could handle a car. The clouds were moving off, and the first glimmer of light showed in a thin sliver along the mountaintops in the east. She began to think in as orderly a way as she could about what

12

might have happened to Charlie. Her father had been so upset, he hadn't told her any details. Maybe he didn't know many. But first there was the question of his horse. Had Charlie been out on his little mare? If he had been, it might be easier to trace him.

"Did they have any details on the news?" she asked the man. "My father called me, but he didn't have time to tell me much."

"What they said on the eleven o'clock news," the man said. "No trace of the boy. Said he disappeared from his home day before yesterday in the afternoon . . ."

"Oh," Jane said, pulling in her breath. "That long ago."

"Yes, ma'am. Said they wasn't alarmed at first because the boy knows the woods and all."

"Yes, he does." I taught him, she thought. We explored the woods together in all the seasons.

"How old of a boy is he, ma'am? I didn't get that."

"He's ten."

"Oh, well then, he's probably going to be all right. Boy that age that knows the woods."

"Do you know if he had his horse with him?"

"Didn't hear nothing about that. I 'spose they would've said so if he did."

"Yes. He usually has her with him."

"A horse is a good friend." He reached for the radio dial. "Local stations ought to be signing on. Might be some news." The radio crackled for a minute, and then the Sons of the Pioneers singing "Tumblin' Tumbleweed" told her she was home again. She'd heard that theme song on the early morning show ever since she was a little girl.

The announcer read a fifteen-second commercial for the drugstore that sponsored the early morning news, and then he went into the news. There was a one-sentence "story" on the situation in the Middle East, a brief story about a thwarted hijacking in Holland, and then some headlines on the local and state news. Jane leaned forward on her seat listening intently, although the volume was up high on the radio.

"No new developments on that missing youngster in the Libby area," the announcer said. "Sheriff, search-and-rescue units, neighbors, and the boy's father are keeping up an intensive search. Sheriff Evans said the possibility of a kidnapping has not been ruled out." He went on to the weather prediction.

"In other words," the driver said, "they don't know."

Jane leaned back, half relieved that there hadn't been anything worse. She went back to thinking about what Charlie might have done. He liked to go off in the woods alone. She always had done that, too. It worried her mother, who believed in the "buddy system" in hiking as well as riding, swimming, and the snow sports. "What if you broke your ankle and couldn't go for help?" she always said. "And nobody would know where you were." Jane's father overruled her, having been a solitary rider and hiker himself all his life; but he did suggest that if they were going far, they leave what he called a flight plan. Then if anything happened, someone would know in general where they were. She wondered if Charlie had filed a flight plan. If he hadn't, he might have forgotten, but more likely it would mean he hadn't intended to go far. He was a pretty conscientious kid. She looked up and saw the driver's eyes in the rearview mirror. He looked so sympathetic, she couldn't stand to face him. She moved a little to get out of the mirror's range. Sympathy meant something bad might have happened or had happened, and she wasn't ready to accept that.

The sun was up over the mountains now, leaving faint streaks of pink behind it. The heavy stands of evergreen were patched with the gold of western larch. A meadowlark sitting on a telephone wire cocked his head at them as they went by.

"Going to be a good day," the driver said. "Still pretty warm and that's a blessing."

"Yes." He means that's a blessing for Charlie, she thought. And of course it was. It was always chilly at night in the woods, even in the summer, but not killing cold. And she had taught Charlie how to keep himself warm if he had to. She pictured him looking for a clump of trees in a sheltered spot, taking his knife, the one she had given him, off his belt and cutting and stripping some poles for a lean-to, covering it with woven boughs. They had done it together any number of times. He'd get together some wood for a fire, and he'd get it started with the metal match that he loved to use. He'd have food with him, if she knew Charlie. And he'd find water without much trouble. They always noticed where the water was when they went for hikes, and Charlie sometimes drank more than he wanted from his canteen just so he could kneel by a stream and refill it. It was hunting season, so he'd be wearing his orange jacket and cap. And maybe by the time she got home, some hunter or one of the rescue party would have seen that jaunty orange cap or heard Charlie's halloo, and he'd already be home in bed, eating everything in sight and ready to tell her the whole story. There'd be some laughs in it, if she knew Charlie. She began to relax a little. That had to be the way it was.

People were already at work on the farms and ranches they passed, doing the things she herself was used to doing—getting feed out for the horses in the corral, taking the dog along to herd the sheep into the pasture where they belonged, feeding the chickens, saddling up to take a look at the cattle out on the range.

The driver slowed down as they came to the small town near the ranch where the Wordens lived. Jane looked for any sign of the unusual, sheriffs gathering or search-and-rescue men or anything out of the ordinary, but there was nothing. Mr. Hood was running up the window shades in his little newsstore. A man in boots and a stetson leaned against the porch of the closed post office. The janitor at City Hall was running up the flags of the United States and Montana. A man on a horse sat quietly at a side road as if he were sleeping. A display of high school athletic trophies in the drugstore window caught the slant of the sun and glinted silver.

Since she had gotten used to towns in New England, it had occurred to her that these little western towns were ugly, but she liked them just the same. She liked to think that westerners didn't pay much attention to their towns because they gave their time and affection to the wilderness. No manmade place could challenge the mountains and the forest and the rivers and lakes, so why try?

Her heart began to pound as they came nearer to the ranch. What would she find? "It's just about three-quarters of a mile up the road," she told the driver. "On the left. There's a wooden sign that says W-Bar-T."

The man nodded and slowed down a little. He turned into the gravel road under the familiar sign that spanned it. Jane tried to make herself relax, but she couldn't keep from sitting on the edge of the seat trying to see ahead beyond the stretch of road.

They came over the rise of the little hill and there was the ranch house, long and low, flanked by two groups of Lombardy poplars. A sheriff's deputy sitting on the porch railing unhooked his heels in a leisurely way and sauntered over to the car. He peered in, shoving his hat back on his head so he could see better. "Yeah?" he said.

"Got Miss Worden here," the driver said, in a voice of authority. He got out and opened the door for Jane and then went around to the trunk to get her suitcase.

Jane looked at the sheriff's man. "Any news?"

"No, ma'am. They're all out looking."

"Is my father with them?"

"Yes, ma'am."

"Is my mother here?"

"No, ma'am. Believe she went to her sister's."

Jane went into the house. It seemed awfully empty. She stood in the wide hall, listening though she didn't know what she expected to hear. Automatically she took off her coat and opened the closet door. Charlie's orange jacket hung on a hook. She stood there looking at it for a long time. When she turned around, she heard the engine of the taxi and remembered she hadn't paid the man. She ran out of the house and called to him.

"What do I owe you?"

"Nothin', ma'am."

"Oh, of course I do. How much?"

He looked uncomfortable. "I'd rather not charge you if you don't mind, Miss Worden. I feel bad I can't join in and help hunt for the little boy, but I got this bad heart, where I'd be more trouble than help. But I'd be pleased not to be paid for bringing you home."

She held out her hand. "Thank you very much. You're very kind."

"Anything I can do, like you need transportation, you or your family, just holler. My name's Skaggs, Pete Skaggs."

"Thank you, Mr. Skaggs. I won't forget."

"Good luck. Keep up your courage." He touched his hat with one finger and drove away.

She went out to the barn. In the corral in back of it she found her own horse, a Morgan named Lady Belle, and Charlie's horse, the little mare he called Lulu. With her arm around Lady Belle's neck, she coaxed Lulu to her and stroked the golden nose with its white blaze. "Where is he, Lulu? Where's Charlie?"

Lulu nickered and turned her head to rub it against Lady Belle's neck.

The sheriff's deputy was back on the porch rail, smoking a cigarette. He reminded Jane of a cover on a western music album.

"Could you tell me about that note or whatever it was?" Jane said. "Could they read any of it?"

It took him some time to frame his answer. "Believe they made out the word 'boy' and 'the' and 'friend.'"

"Friend?" That was puzzling. Kidnappers didn't usually call themselves "friend." "Do you mean it was signed 'friend'?"

"I dunno, ma'am. I didn't see it myself."

"Do you know where they've searched?"

"All over, I believe."

Jane sighed and went into the house. The man was not exactly a gold mine of information. She went upstairs and called her aunt's house on the upstairs phone. It was answered almost immediately.

"Hello?"

"Aunt Mabel? This is Jane."

"Oh, Jane! Where are you?"

"Home. I just got in."

"Is anyone there?"

"Only one of the sheriff's men. How's Mother?"

"Well, she's asleep now. The doctor gave her a shot. She sort of . . . you know . . . collapsed. He was worried about her heart, but it seems to be all right, so far. My dear, why don't you come over here? Don't stay in that house alone."

"I'm going out to look for Charlie."

"Oh. Yes, of course you would." Aunt Mabel's voice broke. "Oh, Jane, it's so . . ."

"I know. But hang in there, Aunt Mabel. It's going to be all right. I know all of Charlie's haunts."

"Yes, if it's a matter of . . . if he just got lost. . . ."

"Look, I'll find him no matter where he is. Trust me."

"Oh, I do, dear. You're the one who can find him if anyone can. But be careful, Janey, promise me to be careful. If he's . . . if anyone else is involved, it could be dangerous. Take your gun."

"I will." It upset her to hear the fear in Aunt Mabel's voice; she was usually so cool and self-possessed. "I'm a pretty tough hombre, you know."

"I know, honey. I'll hang on. I've got to, for your mother."

"Tell Mom to try not to worry."

"She'll be so glad you're home. You were always the competent one, Jane."

"All right, take it easy. I'll call you later."

After Jane hung up, she became aware that the sheriff's deputy was in the hall downstairs. She looked over the bannister. "You'd better stay outside, hadn't you?" she said coldly. "You *are* guarding the house, aren't you?"

He looked disconcerted. "I came in for a drink of water, ma'am. Got kind of thirsty."

"Well, there's water in the kitchen." She turned away, annoyed, and went into her room to change her clothes. She didn't like the idea of being spied on by this character. She wished someone more responsible were looking after things here. What if the kidnapper, if there was a kidnapper, came with another note? This idiot would probably just sit there breaking down the porch rail and chewing on a home-rolled cigarette. There was such a thing as being too darned western.

She put on corduroy saddle pants, boots, a woollen shirt, and a warm sweater. Down in the kitchen she filled her canteen, noticing that the deputy had spilled water on her mother's clean floor. Quickly she put half a loaf of bread, two cans of sardines, and a couple of bananas in a small nylon backpack, and went out to the corral to saddle up her horse. She put her .22 in the saddle holster. For a moment she wondered what she would do if she had to use it. She never had been able to shoot even a rabbit. But rabbits weren't evil; rabbits were no threat to the brother you loved. That might make things different.

She noticed that someone had been feeding the stock recently. She rode over to the front of the house. "Who fed the animals?"

He shrugged. "Dunno. Nobody's been around here since last night. Your pa and them camped out, to save time."

"Well, somebody's fed them. Not you, I suppose?"

"No. Nobody told me to." Suddenly he looked angry. "Could be that breed sneaking around here in the dark. I've drove him off four, five times."

"Who?" she said sharply.

"That half-breed from up the river, lives with his father, Injun mother's dead."

"Do you mean Vic? Victor Barrett?"

"Yeah, that's the one. He drug some of your alfalfa out for the horses. I caught him and drove him off." He looked pleased with himself.

"Don't you ever do that again!" she said. "Vic is our friend." She wheeled her horse suddenly, startling the man so that he almost fell backward off the railing as the horse's hindquarters swung around at him. She touched her heels to Lady Belle's sides, and the horse broke into a fast trot. She was a little ashamed of herself, scaring the man that way, but it enraged her when people were mean to Vic. He was one of the best friends the Wordens had. He worked for her father whenever he needed a hand and many times did little errands and chores for her mother, refusing pay. Vic had taught Jane a lot about the wilderness and about fishing, although he was two years younger than she was. Charlie adored him. She muttered angrily, thinking of that stupid deputy driving Vic away when he was trying to help, probably insulting him, too. Ignorance was almost as bad as deliberate evil.

Glad to be out, Lady Belle broke into an easy gallop as they angled across the meadow toward the forest. The sun shone in a cloudless sky and already the day was warm with an Indian summer softness. It seemed impossible that sad things could happen in weather like this. If it hadn't been for the occasion that had brought her here, she'd have been exultant at being home and out on her horse on such a day.

Almost without thinking it out in advance, she turned

22

the Morgan's head toward a little game trail that led to a cave, an abandoned bear's cave, that was one of Charlie's favorite spots. She doubted if anyone else, except Vic, would know about it.

Even in the woods the sun filtered through, its warmth making the pine needles smell good. Lady Belle stepped on a huge toadstool and shied as it made an almost inaudible pop. Jane laughed and patted the horse's neck. "Silly goose." Lady Belle tossed her mane in response.

She stopped the horse and slid out of the saddle when they came close to the hillside where the cave was. She looped the reins loosely around a tree and ran over to the mouth of the cave. "Charlie? Charlie, are you there?" Her voice sounded strange. She was sorry she'd called out, because the lack of an answer frightened her so badly.

She pulled away the brush that covered the mouth of the cave and peered in cautiously. It was always possible that another bear had discovered it and was taking it over for the winter. She unhooked the little flashlight she wore on her belt and flashed it inside. The torn old tarp that Charlie kept in the cave was there, but it looked as if it had not been used lately. There were leaves scattered over it and dust had blown in. Jane reached in and picked up a paperback book that lay face down on the floor of the cave. *The Adventures of King Arthur.* Charlie must have been reading that for the seventh or eighth time. She put it in the big inside pocket of her parka and went back to her horse.

She sat in the saddle for a minute, thinking. She wanted to make this search methodical—no panic, no disorder. What was the next Charlie-hideout along this route? The broken bridge on the river, where Vic had taught them both to fish. She turned her horse toward the river.

As she rode along, it occurred to her that so far she hadn't run into any of the searchers. They must have beaten the bushes around here and gone further on. Or they might not have come down this particular trail at all. There were no signs of them. It worried her that Charlie's orange jacket was back home in the closet. He shouldn't be out in the hunting season without it. It didn't seem like him to forget it. It was possible the sheriff might have cleared hunters out of these woods, to make the search easier. She hoped so. She was wearing her own orange nylon parka and an old hunting cap of her father's. Normally she stayed away when hunting season was on, because although most local hunters were careful, a lot of. people came in from out of state who didn't necessarily have good sense about hunting. Last year one of them had shot two of her father's best steers from a Jeep with a high-powered rifle. It was not her idea of sport.

The river narrowed and turned just below the half-collapsed footbridge that she was looking for. In the spring the water ran fast and white and could be dangerous, but at this time of year it slowed down and narrowed away from the banks.

She found the bridge. Underneath the half that remained was a good place to stand and cast for fish because there were dark pools where the river made its bend. No one was there. An old creel hung from one of the bridge supports, but it was empty except for a spider who was busily spinning her web from the creel to the bridge. The web, catching some of the moisture from the river, shone in the sun like thin silver filaments. Signs of Charlie—the tarp, the book, the creel—but not recent signs. Although she didn't want to, she called his name.

The chatter of a squirrel stopped for a moment and then went on. She brushed some gnats from her face, and as she turned she saw a pygmy owl perched on a hollow stump staring at her with his round, unblinking eyes. He was only about six inches long. Part of a tiny rodent of some kind lay on the ground below him. Jane had interrupted his lunch. She wished she could ask him if he'd seen Charlie.

The next place she had in mind to check was a small, almost entirely collapsed cabin that she and Charlie had found one day when Charlie had darted off the trail to chase a jack rabbit. The cabin had obviously been deserted for years, but Charlie had been enchanted with it, and afterwards he had propped up one end of it to use as one of his hideaways. She remembered he always kept a spare chocolate bar there, closed up tight in a coffee can. Each time he ate one, he replaced it with another. The cabin was quite some distance into the woods, along a heavily overgrown trail. She had to ride with her head ducked low and her hands ready to catch branches that might strike her in the face. Branches scraped against Lady Belle's sides, and the horse plainly did not enjoy the trail.

Charlie had blazed a tree at the place where one moved off the trail to the cabin. Jane dismounted and tied up Lady Belle. "I'll be right back," she said. She saw that Charlie had hacked away the worst of the brush that had blocked the way, so it was easy to find the cabin once you knew what you were looking for. He had stopped the clearing some feet short of the cabin, however, so that anyone happening upon the little pathway wouldn't be likely to see the cabin itself.

It looked as she remembered it, weatherbeaten and broken down except for Charlie's little shelter. She bent down to look inside. There was a sweater of Charlie's that she recognized, another paperback book, this time an Ellery Queen, an unopened can of peaches, and the coffee can. She opened the can and found a Nestlé's chocolate bar. She put it back and re-covered the can. He'd been coming here, but there was no way to tell how recently.

She straightened up and leaned against a birch tree outside the cabin. Could he have gone fishing further down the river and fallen in? It didn't sound like him. He wasn't the kind of boy who was clumsy or reckless. Charlie knew what he was about.

"Janey."

Her heart almost stopped, and she whipped around expecting for a second to see Charlie, although it was not Charlie's voice. It was Vic. He stood in the shadows in a clump of trees looking at her. She hadn't heard a sound until he spoke.

"Vic," she said. "You scared me. I thought, I don't know why, that it was Charlie."

He came toward her. He looked taller and slimmer than he had when she had last seen him, although that had only been a couple of months ago. He had his mother's dark eyes and straight black hair and his father's fair skin. "Because you wanted it to be Charlie. I'm sorry I scared you. I knew you'd come here."

"You're out looking for Charlie, too."

"Yes. We've all been looking, ever since he disappeared."

"What do you think has happened?"

"Somebody has got him."

She felt a quick twist of pain in her chest at his stark statement. "You don't know that, do you?"

"I know Charlie. So do you. He doesn't get himself lost. He doesn't go out in hunting season in a pair of jeans and a dark blue sweater. He doesn't fall in the river and drown. Not Charlie Worden."

She knew that what he said was true; she had known it all the time. "But who would . . . would kidnap him or whatever?"

He didn't answer for a minute. His forehead wrinkled in a troubled frown. "I don't know—you know, not really. I know of a couple of guys from town who were real mad at your father."

"Who?"

"Chet Eberle and Mitch Donahue."

"Why were they mad?"

"Your father laid them off last month because they fooled around too much on the job. Also he thought they were stealing stuff—tools and stuff like that. And they let some sheep get lost—lost or something."

She tried to remember them. Quite a few men worked for her father in the summer and fall, and she didn't always see them much except when they rode in off the range or hung around the barn. "Do you think they'd do a thing like this?"

Again he thought carefully before he answered. "Mitch Donahue might. I don't think Eberle would. He's too lazy and too much of a drunk to be bothered. No, I don't think he would. He might rip off stuff that was laying around, but I don't see him into any real crime like kidnapping."

They walked up the path to the trail.

"What does Dad think?"

"He's most too worried to think. He's been beating the bushes. He sent me down to Donahue's place, but Donahue's not around."

"Where is he?"

"Eberle says he got a job down at Big Spring."

"Do you believe it?"

Vic shrugged. "I don't know."

"Is the sheriff checking on it?"

"Oh, the sheriff. He likes to think no local boys are going to commit any crimes. It's got to be Indians or hippies or else people from California. He told your father he'd check out Donahue, but I doubt if he did."

She thought of the deputy sheriff at the house. "It was you that fed the stock, wasn't it." He nodded. "And that idiot deputy gave you a bad time."

"Who cares. I just waited till dark to feed them. He was sound asleep by then. Big law man."

"Dad must really be in a state if he forgot to look after the stock."

"I told him I'd do it."

She unhitched Lady Belle and led her back up the trail, Vic following. "I was going to check all of Charlie's favorite places, but you've done that, haven't you. And if he really has been . . . kidnapped, then that's a waste of time anyway." She faced Vic. "You don't think this Donahue would hurt Charlie, do you?"

"He's always been a mean man."

"Vic, what are we going to do?"

Vic thoughtfully stripped a twig with his knife. "I'm not real sure yet. This sheriff, you asked about him. . . . He's not really a bad guy, only he's pretty young and inexperienced. . . ."

"How did he get elected?"

"He looks like a young John Wayne." Vic grinned briefly. "He tries, but he's seen too much TV. He's out now, him and his men, following all the regular trails. If it *is* Mitch that took Charlie, he's not going to march off down one of the regular trails. In this country that's about as smart as walking along Highway 93."

"That's another thing. Why does everybody . . . me included . . . assume that they're in the woods? I thought so at first because if Charlie did get hurt or lost on his own, he'd likely be in the woods. But if he's been kidnapped, this Mitch might just drive him off in a pickup or whatever."

"Yeah, but it'd be pretty easy to find him if he did that. Mitch is smarter than that. And he knows the woods. He was a logger for a while, and sometimes he traps. I guess he'd head for the woods all right, but not where anybody could find him." He shook his head. "I wish they didn't have that mob of people in here. Every time I think I've come across some signs, it turns out it's the sheriff's men or the search-and-rescue guys I'm trailing."

Jane felt heavy with discouragement. She sat down on a stump and took the food out of her knapsack. "Let's eat something. Maybe we can think better."

Vic pulled a worn map out of his hip pocket. "I've

got one of those Forest Service maps of the region. I've been marking off the places I've looked."

"That's good." She felt reassured by Vic's competence and calmness, as he showed her the map. "I figure if you were hiding out, this might be a good section." He pointed to a place on the map. "It's hard to get into, awful brushy and some swamp, but if you work your way in there, there's a stream and good cover. I got a deer in there last year."

"Well, let's go in there." She tossed her banana peel under a tree, where a watching squirrel raced down from his perch and grabbed it, pulling at it with his sharp teeth and keeping a wary watch on them.

"It's not an easy ride."

"Nothing about any of this is easy." She mounted her horse. "We'll take turns riding Lady, all right?"

"I don't mind walking." He gave her a sudden impish grin. "Got a little Indian in me."

Before they left the trail they were on, they twice encountered men from the sheriff's department. They stopped to talk for a minute. The men looked tired and frustrated.

"We made camp last night," one of them said, "to save the trip back to town. Your father was great, Jane. He sat there by the fire telling tall tales to the guys, like nothing had happened."

"He's a pretty terrific guy," she said.

"You can say that again. Those guys that work for him, they're all out with him a hundred percent."

"I'm glad. They're a good bunch."

"Where you kids heading for?"

Vic answered quickly. "Just moseying around, trying

to remember the places Charlie liked to go."

"Good idea." The man stretched and turned to his companion. "Well, come on, Joe, up and at 'em."

In the second group was Jake, her father's foreman. He put his arm around Jane and hugged her. "Glad you made it back here, kid. Keep your chin up."

"Make Dad go home and get some sleep tonight," she said.

"Sure will. Hope it'll all be over by then." He nodded to Vic. "Everything okay with the animals?"

"Yeah, they're fine."

She rode ahead of Vic in silence. The discouragement that she'd felt in the men was contagious. With so many people out hunting for Charlie, how could they all miss him, if he were really out here? But of course the forest was very big. It stretched to the Idaho border and beyond.

"If this Mitch were on the run," she said to Vic, "I suppose he might head out of state."

"Maybe. But kidnapping is a federal offense."

"Has anybody called the FBI in Butte?"

"The sheriff said he was waiting till he was sure it was a kidnapping."

"Good God!" she said. "Why doesn't he get with it? There's been one note. What does he have to have, a . . ." She broke off, realizing she had almost said "a body?"

"I think he'd like to make the arrest himself. Like I said, he wants to be a hero."

"I'd like to talk to this sheriff," she said grimly.

"I imagine your Dad can handle him pretty well."

She rode on, concentrating on the rough going. After a while she had to dismount and lead Lady Belle through thick growth. Vic guided her around a swampy patch and plunged again into thick brush and a stand of small, close-growing pine. She could see the marks of an old forest fire.

From time to time they stopped to rest, but they didn't talk much. The air was warm and close, and Jane took off her parka and her sweater.

"I don't think you'd be likely to find any hunters in here," Vic said, "which is another reason Mitch might go for it. The sheriff is 'sposed to have shut off the area to hunting anyway, since Charlie got lost, but of course there are probably hunters already roaming around that wouldn't know that."

"I hope Daddy is careful."

"Sure he will be."

They waited while Lady Belle drank noisily from a narrow stream. Jane waded in and splashed water on the horse's sides to cool her off.

It was late afternoon when they came to the area that Vic had spoken of. They searched it thoroughly, almost inch by inch. Vic found the ashes of a campfire but it was a long-dead fire, the ashes scattered and blown. He kicked at a charred log. "Well, somebody besides me knows about this place anyway. I wonder who."

"But no sign of Charlie."

"No. I'm sorry, Janey. I got you on a wild goose chase."

"Don't be silly. If we're going to find him, we'll probably run into a lot of dead ends first. It would be pure, blind luck just to walk up on them."

"And risky." He glanced at the gun on her saddle. "Maybe you ought to have that handy, just in case."

Before they started back, she unsheathed the gun and carried it in her hand. "Could you shoot anybody, Vic?"

He thought about it. "I wouldn't want to. Not unless somehow I really had to, to save somebody's life or something."

"I think I could shoot anybody that hurt Charlie," she said.

He looked at her quickly. "That wouldn't do any good."

"It would do me good."

"No. You'd wish you hadn't all your life. You're not the kind of person to go around shooting people."

"I don't know what kind of person I am, but I could shoot anybody that hurt Charlie."

They didn't talk any more. Jane was so tired that when she sat on her horse, she found herself falling asleep and beginning to slide out of the saddle. Twice Vic caught her before she fell.

When they came to a small clearing, he said, "Janey, you take a quick nap. I'll keep watch."

"No, I'm all right."

"No, you're not. You're going to fall off your horse and hurt yourself, and then you won't be anything but a nuisance. You sleep for twenty minutes or so. It'll help."

She was too tired to argue. She lay down on the warm, pine needles and although she meant to say, "call me in twenty minutes," she was asleep before she could say it.

J ane woke with a start. Vic had shaken her gently awake, and he held a warning finger to his lips. She sat up quickly, and he moved to the place where Lady Belle was nibbling half-heartedly at the leaves of a chokecherry bush and put his hand over her nose. Someone was coming.

Jane eased herself back into the cover of the trees, holding her gun ready. She raised it as two men stepped into the clearing, then put it down and jumped to her feet.

"Dad!"

Her father stared at her in amazement. "Janie! Wherever did you . . ." He broke off and put his arms around her as she ran to him. "Oh, am I glad to see you! Bless your heart, baby, I am so glad to see you." He held her off and looked at her, tears in his eyes.

Jane found it hard not to cry. Her father was unshaven and dirty, and he looked so tired, she could hardly bear it. "I'm glad to see you, too."

"When did you get in?"

She told him. "Vic and I have been hunting for Charlie."

He nodded wearily. "The sheriff just checked on his

34

walkie-talkie with the guy at the house. There's nothing new."

For the first time Jane looked at the other man. He smiled at her and nodded. "Howdy," he said. "I'm Sheriff Evans."

She nodded. "How are you."

"I'm trying to get your father home for some sleep," he said. "He's bushed."

"I can see he is. Daddy, let's go home and get some sleep. We both need it."

"How can I sleep," her father began.

"Everybody has to sleep sometime. You're no good to Charlie if you're falling-down tired. Come on."

He hesitated. "George," he said to the sheriff, "you'll keep some men out?"

"Of course I will," the sheriff said. "That's my job."

He's either very sure of himself, Jane thought, or not sure at all and trying to bluff it. She watched him as he checked around with his key men on his walkie-talkie and told them he was going in. He gave orders to keep up the search and check with him every two hours.

"Get word to Jake to round up the boys and bring 'em in by sundown," Jane's father said to the sheriff. He put his hand on Lady Belle's stirrup and nodded to Jane. "Up you go, honey."

"You ride her, Daddy. I'm not nearly as tired as you . . ."

"No, not a chance. I'm fine." He led the horse out onto the trail. "Everything all right at home, Vic?"

"Yes, Mr. Worden, all okay."

He sighed. "I don't know what I'd do without Vic."

"I know," Jane said.

Vic looked self-conscious. "I'll take off now. See you later." He was gone before they could protest.

"He'll go on looking," Jane said.

Her father looked up at her and shook his head. "It's going to be all right, honey. It's got to be. Charlie always lands on his feet."

"I know. I feel that way too."

They were too tired to talk much on the way back. The sheriff walked some distance behind them, now and then stopping to examine something that caught his interest—a cigarette butt, a trampled bush.

"So darned many people out," Jane's father said in a low voice. "The signs don't mean anything. But I guess that's the way it has to be."

"Shouldn't we call the FBI?"

"Yes, that's one reason I'm heading in now. I'm sick of waiting for Evans to do it. He means well, but he's inexperienced. Did you see your mother?"

"She was sleeping. I talked to Aunt Mabel."

"Glad she got to sleep."

They walked on in silence to the ranch house. Jane was not quite so exhausted after her short nap. She wanted to ask her father about Mitch Donahue, but she'd wait till he was home and resting.

The deputy sheriff was stretched out in the canvas hammock on the porch, sound asleep. He didn't even wake up when they came up on the porch.

"Great guard," Jane said, and her father made a face.

The man woke suddenly and jumped up, looking embarrassed. "Just getting in a few winks. I've been on duty since midnight last night."

"Get on home and get some rest," Jane's father said. "We'll be here now."

The guard hesitated. "I'd better wait for the sheriff to tell me . . ."

"Oh, get on along," Mr. Worden said impatiently. "George has got more things to worry about than you."

The deputy looked sulky. He muttered something and started for the old pickup parked out by the barn.

"You forgot your thermos," Jane said, holding it out to him. It smelled faintly of bourbon.

"Did you have something to eat?" Mr. Worden asked. "I guess nobody had time to think about you . . ."

Mollified, the deputy said, "Yeah, Sheriff told me to bring some sandwiches. My wife give me some hot soup." He glanced quickly at Jane, indicating the thermos. "Well, so long. Hope you find the boy."

"Where did the sheriff dig him up?" Jane asked her father as the man walked away.

"God knows. He swore in half a dozen extra men for this. I don't know the man." He turned to go into the house, but he stopped at a shout from the direction of the corral. "Who's that?" He was tense.

"It's Vic."

Victor ran toward them with something in his hand, and the deputy turned and came back, curious to see what had happened. Vic handed a piece of paper to Mr. Worden. "It was pinned to the corral fence."

Mr. Worden reached for it, but his hand was shaking so badly, Jane took the paper, frowned over it a moment, and then read it aloud. "It says: 'IF U WANT TO SEE YR BOY ALIVE, LEAVE 25 THOUSAND IN PAPER SACK UNDER ROCK IN BOYS CAVE BEFORE DARK. FRIEND WILL MAKE PICKUP. NO COPS. ANY INTERFERING AND BOY WILL BE DEAD.' "

Jane and her father stared at each other. Jake and three

of the other hired men were riding across the meadow toward the house, drooping tired on their horses.

"Before dark!" Jane's father glanced at the sky. "I'll need to rout out Henry to get the money from the bank. . . . Janey, call the FBI in Butte, but tell 'em no interference till we get Charlie back." He stopped. "What cave?"

"I know where it is," Vic said.

Jane said, "It's a hideout of Charlie's."

The deputy made a sudden lunge at Vic and grabbed him by the front of his shirt. Vic said, "Hey!" and tried to pull away.

"What do you think you're doing?" Jane said. "Let him alone."

"He's the one you're lookin' for," the man said triumphantly. "He's the 'friend' that's going to pick up the money. Then he'll split with his buddy."

"Don't be a fool, man," Mr. Worden said. "Let the boy go."

"I caught him sneakin' around here four, five times."

Jake rode up to the group. "What's goin' on?"

Mr. Worden said to the deputy, "I haven't got time to argue with you. Let the boy go."

"Oh, no," the deputy said. "I'm the law around here. I'm taking him in."

Moving as fast as a boxer Mr. Worden stepped toward the deputy and punched him hard in the shoulder. The man let go of Vic and staggered back, almost falling. Jake laughed. Then as the deputy's hand moved toward his gunbelt, Jake said sharply, "Get your hand off that gun, cowboy. You better head on home now and tell your boss to send a grown man if he wants to send anybody out here." As the deputy hesitated, Jake stepped toward him. The deputy said something under his breath and left.

"Janey, fill Jake in. I've got to get hold of Henry. Vic, you stick around. We'll need you." He ran into the house.

Jane told Jake, and the other hands who had now joined them, what had happened.

Jake looked anguished. "If he harms that kid. . . ." Then changing his tone he said, "Harve, you've got the fastest car. Go rev 'er up, in case the boss has to get in town fast to pick up the money. Vic, you can show us where the cave is, right?"

"Sure," Vic said.

"I'll call the FBI as soon as Dad's off the phone," Jane said. "And I'd better call Aunt Mabel. Mother might hear it on the radio." She ran into the house. She wasn't sure there was any sense in feeling better, but she did. At least now they had some clue, some hope. Maybe the man, or men, would just pick up the money and let Charlie go. Poor Charlie. He must be pretty scared, although he didn't scare easy.

Her father was just hanging up the phone. "He'll meet me at the bank. Honey, let your mother know, but break it easy."

"Sure. Harve's got his car ready to drive you to the bank."

He grabbed his hat and ran out to the waiting Thunderbird. Jane heard the engine roar as the car raced for the road. She picked up the telephone and asked the operator to get her the FBI in Butte.

Jane's mother sounded faint and anxious, but she caught some of Jane's hopefulness now that something was being done.

"Everybody was just shooting in the dark, Mom," Jane said, "but now we know where it's at. So just hold on. I think we'll be a lot happier tomorrow at this time." She crossed her fingers.

After she had talked to her mother, she got a lot of steaks out of the freezer. The men were still staying around, waiting to see what happened next, waiting to do what more they could, although they were tired. She called in Buddy Flanagan, who sometimes did the cooking for the hands.

"Buddy, want to give me a hand? The guys must be hungry."

"You bet, Janey." He set to work at once peeling potatoes, cutting them up for fries, opening big cans of tomatoes, getting water going for coffee.

"How big a paper sack do you need for twenty-five thousand dollars, do you suppose?" Jane was looking through the stack of neatly folded paper bags that her mother kept in the cupboard.

"Gawd, Janey, I don't know. I never seen even one

thousand dollars. I guess it depends on how big the bills are." He paused, his paring knife poised over a potato. "Twenty-five thousand! That's a lot of loot." Then quickly he added, "But nothin' compared to little old Charlie. That's a great kid, that Charlie." He sighed and sliced the potato expertly.

"Any idea who it could be?"

"Nah. Who would do a rotten thing like that? Must be a stranger."

She made a big salad and set the long table in the kitchen. Then she joined the other men who were waiting outside for Mr. Worden to come back.

They talked about casual things: about Jerry's hive of bees that had swarmed on top of Mrs. Honnicut's chimney; about the high price of bourbon; about whether handmade cigarettes were easier on the lungs than commercial ones, or harder. Jane listened with only a fraction of her attention. She was listening for the roar of Harve's car. The sun was getting low in the sky. Maybe another hour of light.

Then the car came, spitting gravel, zooming to a sudden stop in front of the house. Buddy came running from the kitchen, and Vic hurried from the barn. Jake and the others stood in a tight, waiting knot.

Jane's father got out of the car, holding a satchel. He made a circle of his thumb and forefinger.

"All set," he said. "Get a bag, Janey."

She ran into the kitchen and grabbed the largest of the bags she had sorted out. In front of the watching men Mr. Worden took five packets of bills from the satchel and put them into the paper bag. He folded the excess paper around the contents and secured the whole thing with two wide rubber bands.

"Vic and Jake," he said, "come with me while we plant this thing."

"I can go, Dad, if you're too tired . . ."

"No, honey, you stay here and rustle up some grub." He started toward the corral. "Vic, you ride Charlie's pony, she's fresh."

Jane watched the three of them ride off toward the forest. The other men watched, too, tense and quiet.

"Well," Jane said, "let's get that meal going, Buddy."

All the men came into the kitchen with Buddy and her, as if they felt the need to stay together. She got beer from the refrigerator for them and found a couple of big bags of potato chips.

"My stomach forgets when I last ate," said Billy Foster, the youngest of the men.

They started kidding Buddy for preferring to drink his beer from a glass, an old joke.

"His ma used to go to the Ritz for her beer before he was born," Al Estes said. "Prenatal influence is what they call it."

Buddy just grinned and kept on peeling potatoes. They kidded Jane, too, about the East, about turning into a dude, about Harvard boy friends.

"This Wellesley College," Al said, "I understand they got a great football team. Headed for the Rose Bowl is what I heard."

"Didn't you know?" Billy said. "Janey plays fullback. Right, Janey?"

"Right, man." She knew they were trying to help her over the tension of waiting, and she was touched. They were a super bunch of guys. She thought about asking them if they had any ideas about Eberle and Donahue, but decided not to. She'd known guys to get very worked up about somebody they thought had done something, and occasionally they got rough with him and it turned out he was the wrong one. No use to start a thing like that, especially now.

It seemed forever, but by the clock it was only three-quarters of an hour before she heard the hoofbeats of the returning horses. Buddy heard them at the same moment, and they rushed to the window. The men's talk stopped instantly. There was a pause and then everyone rushed outside.

Everything was all right so far. As they lined up at the kitchen table and began to eat hungrily, the men asked questions and Mr. Worden and Jake answered them. Vic was quiet, as he always was around the men, but they treated him with respect.

When the meal was finished and the men had cleaned up the kitchen, Mr. Worden said, "Any of you guys that want to can go on home. If you want to stick around, there are plenty of bunks. Janey'll find you some sheets and blankets. There's nothing to do now but wait." He sighed. "And that's the hard part."

"That note . . ." Buddy said. "It didn't say when he'd pick up the dough, did it?"

"No. I suppose sometime after dark. I want to talk to the sheriff and make sure he doesn't let anybody near the place." He went into the other room to phone.

It was beginning to get dark. Janey tried to imagine where Charlie was, how he was feeling, but that was a line of thought that was too upsetting.

"Why don't you go to bed, dear?" her father said,

coming back in. "Nothing to do now. We won't dare check out the cave till tomorrow. The FBI guys will be here on the early morning plane, the one you came in on, I guess. I told Evans to get them out here as soon as they come." He pulled his pipe from his pocket and began to fill it. "Evans is kind of sore because I didn't consult him before I took the money out to the cave. What the heck does he think? There wasn't time to sit around and chew the fat with him."

"He doesn't know where the cave is, does he?"

"I wouldn't think so. I didn't know myself. It takes a kid to find a cave."

"Dad, Vic mentioned Eberle and Donahue. He said they had a grudge against you. . . ."

"Eberle's in the clear. The sheriff talked to him. Donahue has left town."

"Do you think? . . ."

"I don't know what I think. But we've got him in mind. Evans is checking him out. Eberle says he's in Big Spring or somewhere."

"Well, get some sleep."

"I will. I've got to unwind first. You get to bed though." He kissed her. "I'm awful glad you're here, honey."

Upstairs she put blankets on the spare beds and checked to make sure they had clean sheets. Then she lay down on her own bed with her clothes still on and fell asleep.

The first slant of light through her bedroom window woke her. She sat up quickly with a sense of fear. The house was quiet except for the running of the shower in the bathroom at the end of the hall. She could smell coffee. In her own bathroom she got out of her uncomfortable clothes and took a quick shower. It was strange to be in the privacy of her own room, instead of in the hustle and racket of the dorm. She, Charlie, her father, and all of them, had been suddenly jerked out of the frame of custom, thrust into an unfamiliar and threatening experience. The daily lives that they took for granted had been swept out from under them. Things like kidnapping had been what you read about in the paper or heard on TV. When it happened in one's own life, one began to think of strange, unnatural things, like shooting the man who hurt one's brother.

In the kitchen she found her father and Jake at the table drinking coffee, while Buddy fried bacon and eggs.

"We'll go out as soon as the sun's up," her father said.

"Mind if I come?"

"No, of course not."

"FBI ought to be in by now," Jake said.

"Yeah. I hope Evans picked them up at the airport."

"Oh, he will," Buddy said. "Evans dotes on authority."

"Including his own," Jake said.

"Oh, he's not a bad guy," Mr. Worden said. "Just overeager. A little carried away with that badge."

They ate their breakfast without much more talk. Then the three saddled up and rode out to the area of the cave. They left their horses and walked single file, silently, toward the cave. Both Mr. Worden and Jake carried guns in their hands. Jane was last in line.

When they were fairly close, Mr. Worden held up his hand for a halt. He stood listening, turning his head slowly in different directions. There was no sound except the sleepy chirping of birds. He motioned Jane to stay where she was, and he and Jake spread out and moved toward the cave from different angles, their guns at the ready position, as if they were stalking a deer, Jane thought.

She saw her father cautiously approach the mouth of the cave and bend down. A moment later she heard his yell of anguish, and her heart nearly burst out of her chest. She thought he had found Charlie dead. She jumped forward to join him and nearly fell over a man who crouched beside a tree, concealed by branches and brush. She screamed and jumped on him. Her father was there in seconds, jerking the man to his feet. It was one of the sheriff's men.

Mr. Worden shook him violently. "What are you doing here? What are you doing here?"

"The . . . the sheriff. . . . Quit shaking me. The sheriff give me orders to stay here and watch all night."

Jake caught up with them. "How did you know about the cave?"

46

"Mort, that guy that was at the house, he trailed you out here so's he could inform the sheriff. Sheriff wanted to catch the kidnapper. He sent me and Marchetti out here to watch."

Mr. Worden waved a piece of torn paper in his face. "You loused it up, you goons, you stupid fools. My boy may be dead."

With shaking hands Jane took the paper from her father's hand. Like the other note it was printed crudely with a felt tip pen. "U TRYED TO TRAP ME U MADE YR CHOISE."

"Is the money gone?"

"Of course it's gone," her father said savagely. "These great lawmen let the kidnapper come right to the cave, pick up the loot, and go . . . with Charlie." He gave the man a fierce shove that nearly knocked him down. "Get out of here. And tell your pinhead sheriff I'll do things my way from here on out."

The man fled.

"Where's the other one?" Jake said.

"Gone, if he knows what's good for him. Or sound asleep in some cozy spot. I hope he rots." Mr. Worden turned on his heel. "Jake, you and I are going after Charlie." Before Jane could speak, he said, "You stay home this time. Go stay with your mother. Have somebody look after the stock and let the rest of the men go home till they hear from me. Whoever stays better sleep in the house, just in case." He was stalking along the path to the horses so fast she had to hurry to keep up.

"I can't just sit there," she said.

"I'm sorry, you can't come. We're going to move very fast." In a softer voice, he said, "You're needed at home."

He slapped his horse. "Come on, Jake." He rode toward the deeper part of the forest, going too fast.

"Keep your fingers crossed," Jake said to her, and loped after his boss.

Jane went over to the cave and looked in. It had been rumpled up a bit. She tried to read in it what had happened. Had Charlie been with him when he came for the money? No, he wouldn't have risked that, with those two sleeping men so near. Charlie would have found some way to signal. By now that terrible man would have discovered that Charlie was hard to handle. Stay cool, Charlie, she prayed, don't make him mad.

She rode back to the ranch and told the men what had happened. They listened in tight-lipped silence. Buddy offered to stay, and then Billy Foster said he wouldn't mind staying. It ended up with all of them deciding to stay, just in case they were needed.

Jane got the Jeep truck out. She tossed some warm clothes into the back, and on second thought went back and got her lightweight sleeping bag, her canteen, and her gun. She knew she wouldn't be able to stand it long just sitting around her aunt's house. She had no plan, but it was better to be prepared. She drove down the gravel loop of road that would take her near Vic's cabin. He should be told what had happened.

He was just coming up the path as she got there. "I was over before," he said, "but Buddy told me you were still asleep." When he heard what had happened, his face darkened with anger. After a minute he said, "Where'll you be? I may want to talk to you." He nodded when she told him. "I got a crazy idea, probably won't work. It was my old man's idea really. It's worth a try." But he wouldn't tell her what it was, because he didn't want to get her hopes up.

She drove the five miles to her aunt's house and went in with a heavy heart. What was she going to tell her mother?

"The truth," Aunt Mabel said, when she had listened to the story. "A mother knows when the truth is being held back from her, and it's much worse than knowing. Let me see if she's awake." She kissed Jane. "You're a good girl, Janey."

In a few minutes she came back. "She's awake and anxious to see you. I told her the news was still . . . well, no news, really."

Jane was shocked at the pallor and strain in her mother's face. "I should have come here first thing," she said, "but I . . . there seemed to be so much to do."

"Oh, dear, I know. You're like your father, not one to sit around and wait patiently." She tried to smile. "All we can do is wait and pray, isn't it."

"I guess so, Mom." Jane looked at her mother's slender hand, held in her own broad, muscular hands. I was never cut out, she thought, to be that sweet and patient. If I can't think of something to do, I'll go crazy.

She was out in the yard playing with Aunt Mabel's two Corgis, when Vic showed up, driving his father's ancient rattletrap car.

"My father wants to see you," he said. "Why don't you come over in your pickup." And he was gone.

Jane was puzzled, but she was ready for any kind of action. She told Aunt Mabel where she was going and took off after Vic, soon catching up with his car's wheezy progress. When she parked the pickup as close

49

as it was possible to get to the cabin, Vic said, "Take the keys."

She followed him down the narrow, rough path to the cabin, which was built in a grove of willows close to the river. She had been here often when she was a kid. She always meant to get over and see Vic's father when she was home from college, but she didn't always make it. He was a man she liked, a tall, rather silent man, with a rare smile. When his Indian wife had died, ten years ago, he had become more withdrawn than ever. He worked at gas stations whenever he could, but he had severe arthritis and it was hard for him to get around.

Vic opened the door for her, and right away the strong smell of whiskey hit her. She was surprised. Mr. Barrett kept the bourbon bottle on hand, and when his arthritis was especially bad he reached for it fairly often, but he was a long way from being a heavy drinker.

But then Jane saw that he was not alone. A man who looked vaguely familiar was sprawled out on a rickety canvas chair, with a bottle on the floor beside him.

"Howdy, Jane." Mr. Barrett held out his hand, with its crippled fingers. " 'Scuse me if I don't get up. The old arthritis is acting up." He smiled up at her. "Have a seat. Son, get Janey a chair. Best one we've got," he said with a twinkle, as Vic pulled up the only other chair in the room, a wicker lawn chair. "Vic found it in the dump and fixed it up for company."

Vic sat down on one of the two low couches, watching his father.

"You know this gentleman, Janey?" Mr. Barrett cocked his head toward the other man. "I invited him out for a friendly drink. Man like me gets lonesome."

50

The man in the canvas chair gave Jane a bleary smile. "I know you," he said.

"This gentleman here is Mr. Chet Eberle. Worked for your father for a short time, I b'lieve." The man laughed and hiccupped. "Real short time." He had trouble with the word "short." "Your pa didn't like us."

Jane stared at him, beginning to understand what Vic and his father were doing. Get Eberle drunk, get him to talk, find out about Donahue. She shot a look at Vic, and he nodded.

"Glad to see you, Mr. Eberle," she said. "How've you been?"

"First rate," he said. "You want a little drink?"

"Sure." Jane got a glass from Mr. Barrett's immaculate little kitchen and let Eberle pour out a jigger of bourbon. "I'll have to put some water in it. I'm not as rugged a drinker as you and Mr. Barrett." She poured about half of it into the sink, and added some water. She came back to the deck chair, sat down, and took a sip. It was cheap bourbon, and even with the water in it, it burned her throat.

"Eb was telling me about his friend Mitch Donahue," Mr. Barrett said.

"Donahue? Do I know him?" Jane asked cautiously.

"Sure you know 'im," Eberle said. "Him and me worked for your old man last summer, me and Mitch did. Old man fired us though. I told Mitch he would. The man ain't stupid. He knows when he's being ripped off." Then he frowned. "That was Mitch, you know, takin' things home. I don't hold with that."

"Of course not," Jane said. She got up and handed

him the bottle as he reached for it and missed.

"Thanks. Always said you was a good kid, Janey. I remember you from when you was a little bitty kid in pigtails."

"Do you really?" She caught the gleam of amusement in Mr. Barrett's eyes. She had never worn pigtails in her life. "You must know my brother Charlie, too."

He scowled at his bottle, and it was a minute before he answered. " 'Course I know Charlie. And I want you to know, Janey . . ." His voice rose sharply and then broke off. He took another drink.

Jane was afraid he was going to pass out before he said anything. She looked at Mr. Barrett.

"I was tellin' Eb," Mr. Barrett said, "I knew you'd appreciate how upset he is about what's happened to Charlie." He paused. "You and your dad."

Eberle suddenly sat bolt upright and began to talk in a fast, loud voice. "I told Mitch it was a crazy thing to do, a crazy bad thing to scare a nice little kid like that. He wanted me to go in it with him. I guess not! I'm not that crazy. I ain't worth much, everybody knows that, but I don't go around heisting little kids for ransom money. 'Chet,' he said to me, 'Chet, you help me out and we go fifty-fifty. Old man Worden's loaded, and we might as well share the wealth.' That's what he said. 'We heist the kid and we demand a hundred grand and we return the kid unharmed, let him go, see, and we take off through Idaho to Spokane, and at Spokane we get a plane to San Francisco, and at Frisco we get a plane to them islands in the South Pacific and we live like kings for the rest of our lives.' " He leaned back and looked at Jane. "I won't say I wasn't tempted. All that hot weather and them dishy Fiji girls . . . Yeah, I was tempted. But hell, I had a kid of my own once. . . . Yeah, I did. He ended up in Deer Lodge, ten years for assault and battery on an officer and stealing a car. . . . He's still there. But I remember him as a little tyke. That's how I like to remember him. He was a cheeky kid but cute. Cute as a button." He slumped back in the chair.

Jane felt a twinge of pity for this derelict of a man still dreaming of his little boy, but it was no time for that. "Do you happen to know what route Mr. Donahue planned to take, Mr. Eberle?" She tried to sound casual.

He looked at her sharply. "You're asking me to rat on my friend, ain't you."

For a moment she didn't know what to say. Then she said, "Yes, I am, because I love my brother Charlie very much."

He sniffed, had another swig from the bottle, wiped his mouth on his sleeve. His eyes were becoming glazed. "I recall young Charlie playin' a trick on old Jake," he said. "Somethin' about hidin' his favorite boots. Jake looked and looked, and finally little old Charlie brought 'em out from the well bucket and said, 'Why, Jake, what a funny place to keep your best boots.' " Eberle gave a long wheezy laugh. "Got a real sense o' 'umor, that kid has." He looked at Jane, making an effort to focus his eyes. "Mind, now, he could change his plans, but what he had in mind was . . . he'd follow the trail that runs parallel to the Kootenai River on the north side into Idaho and come out at Moyie Springs, that's a little dot on the road. He'd buy a car there or Bonner's Ferry, or swipe one if necessary but probably not because that's risky. . . . Then he'd drive down to Spokane, and from there on, fly the friendly skies of United." He sniffed and then decided to blow his nose on a blue bandana. "Or Northwest, or whatever. Ain't never flown myself." He leaned back as if he were exhausted.

Jane got up. "Thank you very much, Mr. Eberle. You won't be sorry."

"Oh, I'll be sorry all right." Eberle closed his eyes. "Always regret what I say when I'm skunked."

Jane took Mr. Barrett's hand in hers. "Thank you and bless you. My father's out looking for Charlie, but the men are at the house. Could you get word to them?"

"Don't worry. I will."

"Ask them not to tell the sheriff yet. Let Vic and me get a head start."

"Don't worry. I knew George Evans . . . when he was a little tyke in pigtails." He smiled at her. "We'll see to it he don't get in there messin' up the trail."

Vic put his hand on his father's shoulder. "You'll be all right, Pop?"

"I was all right before you was ever born. Take care of Janey." With Vic's help he pulled himself up from the chair. "I'll get up the road to the Henleys' phone."

"We'll drop you off."

"No, no, you git goin'. No time to waste." He nodded to Jane. "Bring back my friend Charlie."

Jane and Vic ran for the Jeep.

Vic grabbed a bulging knapsack as they left the porch of the cabin.

"Looks like you were prepared," Jane said.

He grinned, glancing at her own gear in the back of the truck. "Looks like we both were."

"I knew I couldn't just sit there and wait." She slammed the car into gear and turned it around. "Listen, we can get to Idaho a lot faster than they can. If we just take the route that goes to Bonner's Ferry, we'll have time to reconnoiter. . . ."

Vic was poring over the map that had been stuck above the sun visor. "Right. Just keep going. I'll spell you when you get tired."

After a while Jane said, "There's one thing that worries me. If Donahue suspects that Eberle might spill the beans, then he'd change his plan, wouldn't he?"

"I thought of that too. I guess we just keep our fingers crossed."

"I think when we get into Idaho, we'd better ask the state cops to keep an eye out."

She drove fast, but she was a good driver, and the weather was perfect. They made good time. She kept thinking about her father and Jake, plunging through the woods with no real plan. She wished she could tell him what she had found out. But she knew Mr. Barrett would brief her father as soon as he came home. Mr. Barrett, she had learned years ago, knew people's comings and goings with remarkable accuracy. When she was little, she had believed his explanation that he had sensory antennae.

Another thing that worried her was what Donahue was going to do with Charlie. He certainly wasn't going to cart him along to Fiji. But where could he jettison him without arousing suspicion? He'd be stupid to harm him, because that would be an additional, unnecessary crime that he'd be charged with if he was caught. Maybe he'd dump him at the last minute, in the San Francisco airport. It wouldn't be easy to keep Charlie out of sight and silent all that time, though. She kept thinking of things that, from Donahue's point of view, might favor not hurting Charlie, and then thinking of other things that would indicate the best thing would be to get rid of him before they got out of the forest.

"Get rid of him." That was a phrase that you couldn't keep in your mind without driving yourself crazy with worry. She pressed her foot down on the accelerator.

"Watch it," Vic said. "We don't want to get slowed up with a speeding ticket."

"We don't know, do we, whether they're on foot or on a horse. That would make a considerable difference in the speed they'd make."

"I expect they're on Mitch's sorrel," Vic said. "Anyway the horse wasn't around anywhere I could see. 'Course he might have sold him if he was taking off for good."

"Either way, we'll get to the Idaho area before they could. We go into the forest and try to intercept them, right?"

"According to the Forest Service map, there's a logging road that goes in for a way. With the Jeep we ought to be able to handle that."

"Good. That'll speed things up."

On both sides of the road heavy stands of timber towered up. Now and then, when they caught sight of the tallest mountain peaks, they saw the year round snow that capped them. Jane hoped Charlie was warm enough. The nights were cold. Oh, Charlie, Charlie, Charlie. She gripped the steering wheel hard to keep back the tears of worry and frustration.

"Want me to drive?"

"No. I've got to be doing something."

It was late afternoon when they came to the first town in Idaho. It was small, but it had a cafe. They went in and ordered a hot meal, and while they waited for it, Jane went outside to a roadside phone booth.

When she came back, she said, "I had a little trouble convincing the highway patrol I was on the level, but I finally did. They're putting out an all-points bulletin, and they'll keep an eye on car rental places in Bonner's Ferry and all over." She sipped her coffee. "I called my aunt, so Mother won't wonder what's become of me, in case nobody remembers to tell them."

Vic spread the map out on the table between them and traced the logging road with his pencil. "See, we can go clear up to here. That'll be a help. We can sleep there tonight, and then fan out here, see, where there are two trails. We can rejoin at the foot of this hill or

57

mountain or whatever it is."

"I hope I don't get lost. I'm not as good at following a trail as you are. You follow trails nobody but a jack rabbit can see."

"Blaze as you go along, so you won't get lost. I don't think you will anyway. You're good in the woods." He traced the two routes. "Anyway we aren't so far apart here."

As they ate, she made a list of things they needed. "Coffee?"

"I've got some in my pack. But maybe a hunk of bacon. There's a sporting goods store up the street. We can get some of those dried meals hunters use. Maybe some jerky."

She sighed. "Sounds as if we're going to be gone a while."

"I don't think so. But we may not want to take the time to catch fish and stuff like that. If we have enough for, say, four meals, that ought to be safe enough. That Charlie's going to be hungry. Put down chocolate bars."

His assumption that they would find Charlie and that he'd be in shape for a chocolate bar cheered her. Think positive, she said to herself, repeating a favorite phrase of Sadie's. For a second she thought of Sadie and the campus and her own room at college. A life she'd known long ago, a life that now seemed unbelievably dear to her.

When they had bought their provisions, Vic drove the Jeep into the forest along the logging road, which soon became narrow and bumpy. Branches scraped both sides.

"Thank God for four-wheel drive," he said. "But you're going to need a new paint job."

"Who cares." She found herself tensely watching the

woods, although it was hardly possible that Donahue could have gotten this far so soon. She hoped he did have a horse. It ought to be easier on Charlie.

The logging road dwindled out partway up a mountain in a patch of land that had been clear-cut. Vic had to back down the road to the bottom of the hill because there was nowhere to turn around. He muttered under his breath about the practice of clear-cutting. "You'd think they'd learn."

Jane held her breath as he negotiated the last curve and stopped in a cleared place at the base of the hill.

He shut off the engine and looked at his watch. "We might as well make camp here. You can sleep in the back of the truck. We wouldn't get far before dark if we started out on foot from here."

"All right." She would have liked to keep going as long as they could, but she knew he was right. This was the end of the line for the Jeep, and it would be easier to camp here than further along the trail. She set up the little camp stove that her father kept in the back of the truck and lit the Sterno can, while Vic took the bucket to the river that they could hear. She made coffee and then let the stove go out. After their meal in town, neither of them was hungry.

"I'll make some sandwiches in case we get hungry before we go to sleep," Jane said.

"All right, but I'm practically asleep already." He knelt in the bed of the truck, sorting out the things that they should take with them in the morning. Food, coffee, both their canteens, his small hatchet attached to his belt, his sharp hunting knife, Jane's gun. "I think I'll pack that little stove along. It'll save building a fire and letting

59

everybody know we're around."

"Can you carry everything?"

"Sure. I've carried heavier packs than this. Are you going to pack along your sleeping bag?"

"I think so. It's really light. I'm a sissy about sleeping. The ground has so darned many bumps in it." In the back of her mind she had a vague idea that Charlie might be chilled and in need of something warm and comforting like the down-filled sleeping bag. He had not gone out dressed for days and nights in the woods.

"After we get further along," Vic said, "we'd probably better spell each other in sleeping, in case somebody comes along, but I don't think we need to tonight, do you?"

"No. I'm a light sleeper anyway. But you're right, after tonight one of us should stay awake."

They went over the map again in detail, and Jane drew a little map of her own to guide her.

"You take the hatchet, so's you can blaze a trail. And listen, if you do get lost—I don't think you will, but if you should—just stay put and I'll find you."

"Right." She looked at him. "That leaves you without any kind of weapon though. I've got the gun."

"I've got my knife." Vic set up a pine cone about thirty feet away and threw his knife at it. The blade plunged into the exact center of the cone. He grinned. "See what I mean?"

"I see." She spread out the sleeping bag in the truck bed and lay down, looking up at the clear sparkle of stars that showed through the tops of the trees. She yawned. "Vic, are you still going to the university in the fall?"

"Yeah, at Bozeman. I'm going to major in agriculture."

"You gave up on forestry?"

"Yeah. I want to raise kooky kinds of cattle. Like St. Gertrudis, for instance. I tried to get your dad to try some, but he didn't go for it."

"He's conservative."

"Yeah. He did get that Charolais bull, but it up and died on him. Now he says Charolais are unhealthy." He laughed. "I'd like to try some of that buffalo-beef cross too. They say it makes a very economical critter." He stretched out on the pine needles beside the truck. "I like buffalo meat, right by itself. Pop bid on a buffalo after the Moiese roundup, but he didn't bid high enough." He yawned and stretched. "It's not even dark, and I'm almost asleep."

"Go to sleep. You haven't had much lately." In a few minutes she heard his regular breathing. She had thought she would fall to sleep quickly herself, but she didn't. She kept picturing Charlie in different situations, all of them frightening. Charlie hungry, Charlie cold, Charlie hurt . . . Cut it out! she told herself sharply. She began the geologic eras, from the beginning this time. Azoic time. Pre-Cambrian time: a) Archeozoic, b) Proterozoic. Paleozoic era: a) Cambrian, b) Ordovician, c) Silurian, d) Devonian, e) Carboniferous, f) Permian. Mesozoic: a) Triassic, b) Jurassic, c) Cretaceous. Cenozoic: a) Paleocene and Eocene, b) Oligocene, c) Miocene, d) Pliocene, e) Pleistocene, f) Recent. "My God!" she said aloud, "I think I've got it!"

Vic murmured something but didn't awaken. Jane turned on her stomach, burying her head on her arms, but it was a long time before she could get to sleep. She

61

kept thinking about violence, trying to understand it. Against all evidence, she had always felt that if you could just talk to a person, make him be sensible, you could talk him out of violence. Now the feelings that stirred deep in herself made her realize that there was a dark unknown in human beings that had nothing at all to do with reason.

Jane woke half a dozen times during the night, certain she had heard something. But it turned out to be an inquisitive raccoon once, and another time a porcupine lumbering through the brush. She knew they were under surveillance by all sorts of creatures. She had slept out often, and except for the occasional grizzly, she felt no fear of wild animals, but now in the back of her mind was the thought that the wild animal could be a man. She kept her gun within easy reach.

She was already awake when the first chitter of birds began. She got up quietly and got the stove going, trying not to wake Vic, but in a few minutes he was awake too, running down to the river to douse his head in the cold running water.

As quickly as she could with the limited facility of the stove, she fried bacon, toasted some bread, and made coffee. Although she was impatient to get started, she followed Vic's example and ate heartily, so they wouldn't have to bother with food again for a while.

When they started up the trail, she gave one last look at the familiar comfort of the Jeep. Vic had run it a little way off the trail and heaped branches over it so it wouldn't be conspicuous if anyone came along.

They walked fast, anxious to get as much ground covered as possible before the sun heated up. It was still bland, blue-sky, Indian summer weather, and again she thanked the gods of the weather for Charlie's sake.

Vic set a fast pace, and for a while the trail led uphill. Jane found herself breathing hard but she was determined not to slow down. When they came to the fork in the trail where they were to separate and follow the two halves of the long loop, she had to stand still a minute, breathing long, painful breaths, before she could speak.

"Listen, if you get to the rendezvous place before I do, don't worry." She tried to laugh but it hurt. "I ain't as young as I used to be, buster."

He grinned. "It's that dude life you been living."

"I know. Anyway I'll get there as fast as I can. How long do you figure it'll take us? Do you want a sandwich to take with you?"

"No, I can last till then. Shouldn't be more than a couple hours. And listen, Janey, if you got any kind of trouble, any kind at all, fire off your gun twice, fast, okay?"

"All right."

"You may run into hunters, so take it easy."

"You, too."

"Walk quiet." He seemed reluctant to let her go alone. "You sure you'll be all right, Janey?"

"Sure I will." Impulsively she shook hands with him, as if they were setting out on strange, separate journeys. "See you." She walked away quickly, suddenly afraid she was going to lose her nerve.

In a minute she was quite alone. Even the birds were

64

still. The postdawn hours that she had always loved seemed eerie now, threatening. She paced herself so as not to get so out of breath, and she walked quietly, stepping along on the piney trail with light footsteps. Her pack felt comfortable between her shoulders, and the feel of the gun in her hand was reassuring. She listened intently and watched intently, but there was nothing out of the usual. Of course, she reminded herself again, they wouldn't have had time to get this far yet. It might be another day or two before they met. Met! She tried to imagine the meeting. Of course Donahue would have a gun. If she were the one who met him, would she have to shoot it out with him? She could do it, for Charlie. Thank God she was a crack shot. All those years of shooting tin cans off stumps might pay off now.

Once she froze at a sound, but it turned out to be a doe, who was as startled to see her as she was to see it. A little later she heard voices, and she swerved off the trail. Two hunters, gaudy in orange suits, carrying their expensive guns, passed her, arguing about where the best place was to find deer. She hoped the doe would elude them.

About half an hour later, after she had climbed a steep hill and come down into a little valley, she discovered four elk browsing. They lifted their heads and looked at her without alarm.

"You'd better get out of here," she said. "Mankind is abroad, with death in his hands." When she looked back a minute later, they were still there. She began to think about all the killing that goes on in the world: man killing animals, animals killing each other, man killing man. What a stupid waste. At least animals usually killed only to eat, and that was an improvement on killing out of pure meanness.

She walked and walked and walked, trying to stay alert. It was easy to let one's mind wander, and that might be a very bad thing to do. She blazed her trail with tiny nicks so that no one else, unless he was very sharpeyed, would notice the marks.

She began to get hungry, but she didn't want to stop until she met up with Vic. He'd probably be ahead of her anyway. The trail was very uneven, sometimes sharply uphill, then steeply down, then leveling out for a while, but always rough and, unless she was constantly vigilant, easy to lose track of altogether.

She stopped and looked at the map. She ought to be there soon. It seemed as if she had been walking forever. She adjusted the pack, which had grown heavy, and strode up the next hill. With relief she saw the faint outline of the other trail winding toward her own around a big berry patch bisected by a stream. This was the place.

She ran down the last short distance and heaved her pack to the ground, rubbing her shoulders in relief. Hearing a sound behind her, she turned around, saying, "Vic? . . ." She froze with horror and screamed.

Standing on the path she had just come down, an enormous grizzly bear faced her, slowly wagging his head back and forth between the big humped shoulders. She looked around desperately for a tree but there was none close to her in this open patch of ground, and she knew better than to run. A bear of that size could easily pull her down from a tree anyway.

Then she heard Vic's quiet voice behind her. "Just stand still, Janey. Stand perfectly still." He was beside her now, speaking soothingly to her and at the bear. "He won't hurt you. He's just curious, right, old bear? Just smelling around to see if we're enemies or not. Relax, Janey, don't be scared. They can smell fear, and they don't like it."

After what seemed a hundred years the bear reared up on his hind legs and peered at them with his nearsighted eyes, then swung around and went back up the trail.

Jane was shaking. "I'm so ashamed of screaming," she said. "Of all the things to do. . . ."

"That's all right. You're nerved up because you keep thinking you'll run into Charlie and Donahue."

"I don't usually . . ."

He interrupted her. "Listen, I know you don't. I'm

Vic, remember? I've known you like fifteen years. I know you're not a screamer. Let's get out of the bear's berry patch before he decides to come back." As they crossed the open ground, he said, "He probably followed you down the trail. They do that."

"Eek," she said, shivering at the thought. But what frightened her even more was that she had panicked. If she lost her cool like that over a bear, what would she do if she encountered Donahue? She'd seen grizzlies before, though never that close. She knew they were unlikely to hurt you unless you scared them . . . so what had she done? Screamed! The thing most likely to scare him. She was disgusted with herself.

"Forget it," Vic said a little later, as they sat beside the river eating sandwiches.

But she found herself glancing over her shoulder every few minutes. I'm turning into a sissy dude, she thought.

"We may as well go along the river till dark," Vic said. "As far as I can see on the map, there's only the one trail along here, as far as this waterfall." He showed her on the map. "We ought to make that by dark. Then tomorrow there's this trail that angles off to the north a little, and two others, one that goes real far south and I wouldn't think they'd be on that one, but maybe this one here. So we'll stay together now, and split up again tomorrow, all right?"

"Sure. Fine." She was secretly glad that she wouldn't have to travel alone for the rest of the afternoon.

They refilled their canteens, washed up, and set out single file along the river trail. She was in the lead, and she set a faster pace than she had earlier, because she wanted Vic to think she could keep going at a good steady rate. As a matter of fact it began to seem easier as the afternoon wore on, as if she had gotten her second wind. The path for the most part was clear enough so she could keep a regular stride, which was a lot easier than having to slow down over and over again because of obstructions in the path. The Forest Service must have been working on this trail, or maybe the Job Corps.

It was still light when they reached the waterfall, which tumbled into a tributary stream that joined the river. They stood under it, catching some of the cool spray, listening to the steady thunder. While they were there, two deer came down to the stream below the falls and drank daintily from the fast-moving water. They had seen no more hunters, but once Vic had pointed off to the north at the sound of gunfire.

They found a sheltered place for camp away from the river, up close to the base of a small mountain with heavy rock extrusions at its base. It was colder than it had been, especially in the shadow of the mountain, and it would have been nice to have a fire, but they agreed it was dangerous. Too easy for others to spot a fire.

Vic cooked some of the freeze-dried beef-and-noodles he'd picked up at the sporting goods store, and Jane made coffee, boiling water in one of the nested stainless steel pans and dumping in some coffee grounds. They had dried apricots and a candy bar for dessert.

Vic peered up at the puffy white clouds heaped up high over their heads. "Rain before morning," he said. "Maybe colder." He got his knife and his hatchet and set about making a bivouac. He shook his head at Jane's offer of help. "Won't take a minute." Neatly and quickly he lopped off boughs and found some fallen birch bark.

He stripped limbs from a pine that grew close to the rock, and sharpened each end of the strongest ones. He shoved one end of the poles into the ground and secured the other in the bark of the pine, until he had a three-pronged frame. This he draped with branches and bark. At the point where the three poles came together against the tree, he lashed the tree and the poles with the rope he wore around his belt.

"There," he said. "Let the rain come down."

She was impressed. "That was neat. I've made shelters, but they never turn out that good."

He looked it over critically and moved a piece of bark tucked in between the interwoven branches. "When you're ready to sleep, hang your parka over the entrance for a door. It'll keep out the rain."

"What about you?"

"Oh, I'll fix me a little shelter." He grinned. "Indians never get wet."

"When I was younger, I used to think I'd give anything to be an Indian."

"The Indian part of me seems kind of far off, on account of my mother dying so long ago and me living with Pop like white people. I'd like to know more about my Indian part, but my mother's folks kind of forgot about her when she married a white man."

"Were they angry?"

"Oh, I don't think so. It happens all the time. But they just sort of put her out of their minds, I guess, like somebody in the family that's gone to live in a far-off part of the world." He pulled down a branch from another tree and pinned it to the ground with a rock. It made a partial shelter. He sat inside it with his back to the tree. "Cozy. I went up to the reservation a couple times to look up my relatives. They were polite to me, but I don't think they gave me much thought."

The first rain drops began to splatter against the rocky hillside. Jane put her nylon hunting cap on. It had begun to get dark suddenly, but she wasn't quite ready for sleep. She picked up a chunk of rock that had broken off the hillside. "Igneous," she said.

The sky blackened, and there was a tremendous clap of thunder. Big hailstones began to fall. Jane dove for her bivouac. "Get in here, Vic," she called. He came in after her. They left the opening empty so they could watch the storm. Hailstones bounced off the roof of the shelter and now and then one fell through to the inside. It was very dark outside except for an occasional flash of lightning. Vic sat with his arms around his knees, watching with delight.

"Crazy about hailstorms," he shouted above the racket.

She laughed, but she was thinking of Charlie, hoping that man had found or made some kind of shelter. Some of those hailstones were big enough to hurt a person, even kill if they hit right.

The storm stopped as abruptly as it had begun, but a light, silent rain went on falling. Vic went outside and found that the limb he had anchored for his own shelter had blown loose. He caught it again in a shower of raindrops from the branches. He piled other branches on the ground for a mattress and covered them with his lightweight "space" blanket.

When she was sure Vic was all right, Jane hung up her parka, leaving a thin space "for fresh air" as she told herself, although she knew she was doing it because it made her feel claustrophobic to shut herself in entirely. There was plenty of air and occasional drops of rain coming through her thatched roof, but it was a reasonably snug little house. She was glad she had her sleeping bag, because the air had turned cold. Vic had agreed to wake her for her watch at three o'clock. Tomorrow with any luck they would find Charlie.

Daylight came reluctantly. The rain had stopped, but the skies were dense and gray, and it was colder. Vic was doing push-ups to get warm. He had already gone for water and had some boiling for coffee. Jane used some of the last of the powdered eggs to make scrambled eggs. "It's jerky for lunch today," she said. "We're out of bread."

"Jerky's better for us. More energy. Pop makes good jerky."

"I know."

He took apart her shelter and left the boughs strewn around as if a storm had blown them down. "Keep dry?"

"Sure. It was a dandy house."

While he was eating breakfast, Vic said, "Did you hear the helicopter?"

She looked up quickly. "No. When?"

"Right when it was getting light. I expect they're out looking."

"Gosh, they can't see much, can they? These woods are so thick."

"Well, they could spot smoke, for one thing. And then there are the open places." He studied the map again. "You take this trail here." He showed her. "It's not so much up and down. But there's a slough in here, so watch out for that. You'll probably find a whole lot of little game trails kind of coming together where the animals scoot around the slough. But keep your eyes peeled." He looked up at her. "We might find 'em today."

"Yes, that's what I figured." She stared at the map as if willing it to show her what was there.

"Remember, two shots if you need me, about ten seconds apart. Then wait five minutes and repeat. Got it?"

"Yes. What if you want to signal me?"

"I'll build a fire. So watch for smoke, only keep in mind where my trail goes, if you can, so you'll have a pretty good idea if it's me or not." He frowned. " 'Course you're likely not to see it from the ground. Well, supposing you get to the rendezvous place, and by the way, it's this little lake here, see? All right, so you get there, and I don't show up and don't show up. Then I guess the best thing would be for you to start backtracking along my trail. See?"

She nodded. "It worries me that you don't have a gun. This guy is going to be armed."

"I know, but I'm a pretty sneaky type. And I've got a knife, plus a hatchet, plus a rope. I'll be all right."

"You be careful though." It really worried her. "You don't think we should stick together today?"

"If we do, we could miss them. Either one of those trails is possible. We ought to cover them both."

She knew he was right, but she wished they didn't have to split up. She had begun to feel convinced, although she fought against it, that she wouldn't find Charlie alive. When she thought of it, a blind rage shook her until she couldn't think at all.

"Do you think he's dead?" she said.

Vic looked up from the backpack that he was strapping up. "Janey, don't start thinking that. We're assuming Charlie is alive. We're hunting for him. We're going to find him."

At least for the moment his calm assurance made her feel better. There was no way of knowing whether Charlie was alive or not, but as long as there was a chance that he was, then she must act as if he was.

"Well, give me a hand with my pack, will you, and off we go." She smiled at him. "I sound like a sissy, but I'll be all right, so don't worry."

"I don't worry about you, Janey." When they came to the place where they were to separate, he waved. "See you."

"Right. Good luck." She watched him bound down the trail, wondering what she meant by "good luck." She wriggled her shoulders to move the pack a little, and started along her trail. Her back and legs ached from yesterday's long hike and the damp night on the ground. The sleeping bag was a great help, but it wasn't like her own bed with its electric blanket. I'm getting soft, she thought—all that eastern living. But she had never really loved sleeping out the way Charlie did. She liked being there, especially on a clear night when you could stare up at the stars and listen to all the little sounds of the forest, but she was fond of comfort when she slept. Her father had gotten her an air mattress, but that was such a lot of bother. She'd given it to Charlie, who had used it as a raft in the river, until the day it snagged on a hidden root.

She walked with extra caution today, more concerned with what she might see than with making time. If Vic got to the lake first, it wouldn't matter. He'd either wait or come back looking for her. She wished they could have stayed within hailing distance.

Every now and then a tree branch released a shower of last night's rain on her head as she brushed past it. The forest smelled good.

She remembered her remark to Vic a day or two ago—it seemed like years ago—that if Donahue had harmed Charlie, she would shoot him. Had she meant she would kill him? She didn't know what she had meant. But now she thought of it as a real possibility. If the man had killed Charlie, had *killed Charlie*, she was pretty sure she would kill him if she could. A man like that had no right to go on living. Even if he went to court and was convicted, he'd get out on good behavior and pretty soon he'd harm someone else. She knew what her parents reactions would be to her even having such a thought. "Things like that don't happen," her mother always said when something horrible happened. "People don't do such things." Her father knew they did, all right, but he was a stickler for the law. He'd studied law before he'd decided on ranching, and it was part of his way of life, his character. But the law wasn't God. The law could be twisted and corrupted and often was. Didn't the Bible say "an eye for an eye and a tooth for a tooth"? Of course it said, "thou shalt not kill," too. You couldn't go by anything really except your own sense of what you ought to do.

The trail widened and became easier to follow. Also easier to happen upon someone unexpectedly. She kept close to the most heavily wooded side. She felt like a hunter stalking his prey.

Toward noon she heard the helicopter. It was flying low, circling. She was near a meadow, so she sat down on a rock to wait till the helicopter went on, and also to rest. She pulled out a piece of jerky and chewed on it. Jerky was not her idea of a gourmet lunch, but it provided the needed energy. She had a long drink of cold water from the canteen.

Another part of her mind took up the argument. No, you couldn't just kill somebody, because there would be so many repercussions for your family. They'd have to go through the agony of seeing you arrested and tried and probably convicted. All that on top of losing their boy. You couldn't do that to them. Unless you killed Donahue and then killed yourself. That would grieve them, but it wouldn't be the long drawn-out agony and shame.

She got up impatiently. "I'm losing my mind," she said aloud. "What kind of a thing is this to be weighing and analyzing? It's insane. Just find Charlie and save him and shut up. You're supposed to be civilized. Whatever that meant. It was not a very civilized world, when you came right down to it."

She crossed the meadow and entered the woods on the far side, trying not to think at all. But a person has to think about something. She was pretty sick of geologic eras and Italian vocabulary. She thought about Sadie and the others, but that was like thinking about characters in a story.

Suddenly she stopped and moved quickly into the trees. She thought she had heard a yell. She listened intently, but there was nothing more. She might have imagined it. Or it might have been the cry of some bird or animal. Whatever it had been, it had seemed to be a cry of pain. After a long wait, when nothing else occurred, she moved very quietly and carefully along the edge of the trail again. Finally she decided it had been some small animal, a rabbit or something, attacked by a larger one.

She crossed a stream, slipping on a log used as a stepping-stone and getting her feet wet. She'd run out of dry socks. Tonight she'd wash some out and dry them by the stove. She picked up the trail on the other side of the stream, but in a few minutes there were several game trails clustered close together. She remembered the slough. It was impossible to tell one trail from another, but they were all going in roughly the same circling direction. She followed them cautiously. She didn't relish the idea of slipping into treacherous muskeg.

She skirted a small pond on the edge of the slough, which was obviously much used as a watering place. There were tracks of deer, elk, and black bear, and a network of tracks of smaller animals. On the far side of the pond a pair of goldeneye ducks splashed up from the surface and flew off out of sight.

She was getting more tired than she had the day before. There was no sun to cheer her up, either. The sky looked like more rain, but so far it had held off. She forced her feet along the trail.

Once from the crest of a hill she saw three pronghorns down in a little valley. They seemed to sense her presence, although the wind was in the opposite direction. Their heads went up almost in unison, and they bounded away with their light, graceful motion.

She slogged on in boggy ground for a long time, until at last the ground began to rise and the footing was firmer. Then she sat down to rest for a few minutes. In her inside pocket she found a package of raisins. She ate them slowly, leaning back against the rough bark of a yellow pine and stretching out her aching legs to ease the muscles. She was so tired, it was hard to think straight.

The clouds in the late afternoon sky were thinning, and there was a slice of blue in the east. She looked at the map. As nearly as she could tell, she was close to the place where she and Vic would meet. The trails were close together in this last stretch. It worried her to look at the map; there were so many little trails Donahue could take. She and Vic might miss him altogether. Charlie, Charlie, where are you? She wished she knew more about Donahue. She tried to remember him, but she couldn't. She wouldn't have recognized Eberle if Mr. Barrett hadn't named him. There were always so many men around the ranch in the summer and early fall. If only she knew what kind of man he was. Was he the type to stick to his original plan, or one who would improvise? Would he panic when he heard the helicopter? And most of all, was he capable of harming Charlie, even killing him, or was he just a reckless man out to make himself some money and get even with his ex-boss? The questions whirled and buzzed in her weary mind.

And for that matter, she thought, pulling herself to her feet, what kind of person am I? Last week she would have said she knew pretty well who she was, but that was probably because nothing had happened to test her.

It was very frightening to be thrown into a situation where she couldn't be sure of her own reactions. If Donahue stepped out onto the trail in front of her right now, what would she do? She tried to walk a little faster, anxious for Vic's company.

The faint sound of her own footsteps began to get on her nerves. Maybe she and Vic were chasing a will-o'-the-wisp. Maybe Donahue was already in Idaho. With Charlie? Or without Charlie? Perhaps they had been wrong to rush off on their own, without waiting for the sheriff. Still, the helicopter overhead made it seem likely that the law was out searching. After all, the FBI was into the act by this time.

She half walked, half staggered down a steep slope. Below her, in the near distance, she saw the shimmer of a pond or lake. She prayed it would be the lake where she was to meet Vic. Maybe he was already there. She wanted to call to him, but that was silly.

Now she could see a clearing between the small lake and where she was. This had to be the lake—there was no other marked on the map. She felt immensely relieved.

A sound like a gunshot brought her to a sudden stop. At first she thought of Vic, then remembered he had no gun. There was another shot, unmistakable, not far. Probably some hunter, but she wasn't going to risk moving into open ground and being mistaken for a deer. She waited, easing out of her backpack. She hoped no idiot was shooting at Vic by mistake.

She moved cautiously to the edge of the trees to see what was happening. A small figure ran into the opening on the lake side, and there was another shot. The figure stumbled and fell and lay still. A riderless horse cantered into sight and wheeled around to the lakeshore trail. A man carrying a gun appeared, running. He aimed his gun at the still body of Charlie.

"Charlie!" Jane's scream jerked the man around toward her, his gun up.

Jane fired over his head. "Put your gun on the ground, Donahue." She walked toward him, her gun leveled at his chest. Charlie lay still, a pool of blood forming slowly beside his head.

"Put your gun on the ground," she said again, in a voice she had never heard before. Her hands were steady, and she felt icy cold. "Get your hands up." It sounded like a western movie. For a fraction of a second she thought of Sadie, saw her smiling face quite plainly, and then it was gone.

Donahue, who looked like any of dozens of tall, skinny cowmen she'd seen in her life, slowly put his gun on the ground and raised his hands, keeping his eyes on her.

She raised her gun and shot it off twice. Vic would come now. But it didn't matter any longer. She was going to kill this man who had just killed her brother. She aimed at his head.

"Listen," the man said. He sounded scared. "I didn't mean to hit him. It was an accident. He give me so much trouble, runnin' away all the time. I wanted to scare him."

She sighted carefully along the gun barrel.

"Don't be crazy," he said. "You're acting crazy."

"You just killed my brother."

"I didn't mean to do it. He was running away with my horse."

"I hate you," she said.

The man screamed, a weird sound like an animal.

Vic ran down the slope at full speed. "Jane! No!" He flung himself at Donahue, tackling him around the knees. She got a clear view of Donahue's forehead and pressed the trigger.

But as she fired, the two men went down together, and the bullet went through the air inches from Vic's shoulder and buried itself in the side of the hill.

For a moment she stood still, trembling violently, watching the two men fight. She had come so close to hitting Vic. She felt dizzy and cold, as if she were suffering from shock.

Vic grabbed a rock and hit Donahue on the head, knocking him out, then swiftly bound him with his rope. He stood up, then, blood on his cheek, and his left sleeve ripped to the shoulder.

"That'll hold him for a while," he said grimly. He ran to the still form of Charlie sprawled on the ground on his face. Jane knelt beside Charlie looking down at him. There was a pool of blood spreading from under Charlie's shoulder. Vic put his head down close to Charlie's face. He slipped his hand very gently under Charlie's chest. Jane began to cry silently. Charlie looked so small.

Vic looked up at her with a sudden shine in his eyes. "Charlie's alive!"

"Alive?" Her mind rejected the word. She couldn't let herself think he was alive and then have to suffer the fact of his death all over again. "Alive?"

Vic had his fingers on Charlie's pulse. "Yes, he is. His pulse is faint, but it's going." He straightened up. "Cover him with your sleeping bag. Don't move him. Keep him as warm as you can. I'll build a fire to signal the helicopter." He ran to the middle of the clearing and began scooping up all the loose brush and bark and piling it into a little cairn of rocks.

Jane ran for her backpack to get her sleeping bag. Alive, alive, alive! Maybe they could save him, save Charlie. She stumbled over an exposed root and almost fell. She was shaking all over. She ran back and knelt again beside Charlie, very gently and tenderly arranging the warm sleeping bag around him. She wished she could get it under him, but she knew better than to move him. She tried to see where the blood was coming from that was seeping into the ground. She couldn't tell for sure because of the amount of it, but it looked as if the bullet, or one of them, had hit in the shoulder on the left side. If it had managed to miss the heart. . . . She sat back on her heels and wiped the sweat from her forehead.

"Charlie, Charlie, hold on. Vic will get help. We'll get you to the hospital. Hold on, old boy. I'm here. Vic's here. You'll be safe now."

His face was frighteningly white, and every now and then his eyelid twitched. She longed to do something for him, get him a drink of water, make him more comfortable, wipe away the blood. . . . But she knew it was dangerous to do any of those things. She could only wait now.

Vic had a blazing fire going, and he was piling on green boughs to make a lot of smoke. He used his still damp flannel shirt to force the smoke up in a series of three puffs, for an SOS. "Get more boughs," he shouted to Jane. "Green ones, damp ones. Hurry."

He hung over the fire, making it do what he wanted

it to do. Sweat poured down his face, and his hair hung in straight, dank strands. Jane brought all the loose boughs she could find that were still green, and then with his hatchet she cut new ones.

Every few minutes she went to Charlie to check on his condition. It didn't seem to change. His lips had parted a little, and by holding her hand close to his mouth she could feel the faint breath. "Oh, Charlie, I know you can't hear me, but hang on, kid, hang on. We're going to get you out of here."

Donahue had recovered from the blow on the head, but after a futile try at loosening Vic's rope, he lay still, staring up at the rising smoke.

Afterward neither Vic nor Jane could remember how long it was before they heard, at last, the wonderful sound of the helicopter. As it flew in over the field, they jumped up and down and waved their arms and yelled.

There wasn't room for all of them in the 'copter, so Vic stayed behind, to return to the Jeep on foot, or by horseback if he could catch Donahue's horse.

When the helicopter pilot and Vic had carefully put Charlie on a stretcher and into the helicopter, and Donahue, handcuffed, was aboard, Jane turned to Vic. "I hate to have you make that long trek back. This guy would come back for you if you wait."

He shook his head. "This time I got wings on my feet." He grabbed her hand and shook it hard. "We did it, Janey. He's going to be all right, I know it in my bones."

"You and your Indian bones." She tried to smile at him.

"Get aboard," he said. "You're holding up the show."

84

Jane sat in the back of the helicopter beside Charlie, her hand on his wrist. She tried to count his pulse, but she was too nervous. It was faint, but it did beat steadily under her fingers. Maybe he was going to be all right. He had to be all right. She watched him anxiously, wondering if he was bleeding internally.

The back of Donahue's head was directly in front of her. The pilot and Vic had bound his hands and ankles securely, and he sat slumped, not moving or speaking. She looked at him with hatred, still wanting to hurt him, kill him. Then she looked away and down at the top of the trees as the helicopter swung around over the forest toward Montana.

Finally she stared at the man's head again, unable to resist, and tried to imagine shooting at that head. With a sudden wrenching vividness she saw in her mind that head split open, the shattered bone, the blood. She closed her eyes tight, trying to wipe out the image. My God, she thought, what have I been thinking of? What did I almost do?

Only last month she had written an impassioned paper for one of her instructors on American violence: violence in the streets; brutality toward those who were in any way different—Attica, Kent State, Jackson State, the Boston school situation; random murders; "thrill" murders—Manson, Dallas; and she had written about the reflection of that violence in the television and movies and books of our culture. She had questioned its roots, deplored it. And yet . . . and yet she had just been close to committing an act of deadly violence herself. She had teetered perilously on the edge of that pit.

She looked down at Charlie's face. It was still and

pale but somehow calm. Charlie would have been horrified if she had shot anyone, even someone who had harmed him. He wouldn't have understood it. Charlie liked things orderly, the way their father did.

She realized she had been holding her breath. Her ribs hurt. She let the long sigh out and relaxed a little. She had barely escaped something very terrible. She tightened her fingers a little on Charlie's wrist. He moved his head slightly, but he didn't open his eyes. It seemed like a good sign, however, that there had been any movement at all in that quiet face. Life was the thing she should use all her energy for, not death, not suffering and agony. It was the only way you could keep yourself alive. The other way, you might as well be dead, even if you were still walking around. Peace and life, not war and violence. It seemed so clear to her now. She felt as if she had come out of a fever. She sat limp and tired.

The helicopter let down gently on the field behind the hospital. The door was opened. Hands reached in for Charlie. Everything was under control.

She sat beside her father in the waiting room at the hospital. It seemed as if they had been there forever. From time to time they tried to talk to each other, to stop themselves from staring at the door through which the doctor would come, and from listening with painful intentness for every footstep. Jane told him briefly what she and Vic had done, but she couldn't bring herself to tell him that she had tried to kill Donahue. Now, back in town, it was hard for her to believe.

"Lucky the helicopter was around," her father said. "You'd have been up a crick, trying to get help way out there."

"We hadn't thought about Charlie's needing to get to a hospital. Vic thought we could handle Donahue between us, with a rope and a gun and all. I guess it wouldn't have been easy though." She frowned, thinking about it. "All we could think about was finding Charlie."

"I know. I was the same. I rushed off like a chicken with her head off. It took me a couple of hours to calm down and make some plans. Well . . ." He looked again at the door. "I wish Doc would hurry it up." He got up restlessly and went out into the corridor.

What would be happening now, Jane wondered, if

the shot she had fired at Donahue had hit him? Worse, what if it had hit Vic? Again she wondered how she could have done such a reckless thing. She thought of the blind fury that had closed down over her mind when she saw Charlie lying there, presumably dead. She looked down at her hands—hands that wrote out answers to college exams, that lifted a coffee cup at a dormitory tea while she listened to talk about Yeats's symbolism, hands that played the piano moderately well—hands that had raised a gun, pressed a trigger. She shivered. Maybe the self was like geologic strata, layers and layers, built up through all the millenia of life. She was going to have to examine those layers of herself much more carefully, recognize them, learn to keep them under some kind of control. Because one thing she was sure of was that no way, no way, was violence and killing the answer to violence and killing. Yet what was? That was the real question. And for that she had no answer.

She knew that when she got back to the civilizing atmosphere of college, where people behaved most of the time pretty much the way they were expected to, it would be easy to put this whole strange and disturbing interlude out of her mind. If Charlie came out of this all right, she would be so relieved, she might forget the murderous rage she was capable of. But she must not forget it. She must look at college and her friends and the everyday world in a different light, because now she knew they could be lost if she wasn't careful. She'd never take them for granted again.

She jumped to her feet as her father and Dr. Mondale came through the door. She knew from the broad smile on her father's face that Charlie was going to be all right.

J ane waited impatiently for the long distance call to go through. She heard Pat's voice answer the corridor phone and the operator say, "There is a person-to-person call for Sadie Libman. Is she there, please?" Another long wait. And then Sadie's voice, sounding wonderful.

"Sadie, it's me. Jane."

Sadie howled with delight, and then said, "Me, Tarzan."

"Everything's all right!"

"I know! It was in the *Boston Globe*. You're famous. How does Charlie feel?"

"He's still in the hospital, but he's sitting up and, you know Charlie, eating. He looks awfully thin and white, but he's going to make it. There'll be some problem with his left arm—the muscles and nerves got torn up—but he'll have therapy, and . . . oh, Sadie, that bullet went so close to his heart . . . I can't even talk about it."

"Don't even think about it. He's safe. When are you coming back? I can't wait to hear it all from the horse's mouth, you should excuse the expression."

"I'll be at Logan Sunday night at six thirty-five."

"I'll be there, duck."

89

"I could take a cab . . ."

"What, and make me miss my chance of getting the big story first? Don't be ridiculous. What airline?"

"Northwest."

"Right on. Bring back some rocks. I'm getting sick of the ones in the geology lab."

"You don't even take geology."

"I know. But at transcontinental rates I'm always tempted to talk nonsense. See you Sunday, kiddo."

Jane said good-bye and hung up. Now she had nothing much to worry about except that stupid geology test. And whether the boy from Cambridge had called; she'd forgotten to ask Sadie. Oh well, there were fish aplenty in the Cambridge sea. She went downstairs to help her mother get dinner for the hands. And later she would make a chocolate chiffon pie for Charlie. He'd requested it.